This Spells Trouble

Paul Collins is the author of many books for children and adults. His writing has won the William Atheling, Aurealis, A. Bertram Chandler, Leila St John and Peter McNamara awards. Paul published Australia's first fantasy novels in the early 1980s. He returned to publishing books in 2007; he has since published around 150 books for children through to young adults. www.paulcollins.com.au

Sean McMullen is the winner of many Australian and international awards, and is a former Hugo nominee. He has written over a hundred adult and young adult works and been translated into over a dozen languages.

Also by Paul Collins
The Jelindel Chronicles
James Gong: The Chinese Dragon
The Quentaris Chronicles (with Michael Pryor)
Rich & Rare (ed)

Also by Sean McMullen
Generation Nemesis
Before the Storm
Changing Yesterday
The Warlock's Child series

THIS SPELLS TROUBLE

Paul Collins and Sean McMullen

FORD ST

First published by Ford Street Publishing, Melbourne

This publication is copyright. Apart from any use as permitted under the Copyright Act 1968, no part may be reproduced by any process without prior written permission from the publisher. Requests and enquiries concerning reproduction should be addressed to Ford Street Publishing Pty Ltd, 162 Hoddle Street, Abbotsford, Vic 3067, Australia.

www.fordstreetpublishing.com

First published 2023

2 4 6 8 10 9 7 5 3 1

Text copyright © Paul Collins & Sean McMullen 2023

Cover design and map: Matt Lin © Ford Street Publishing

ISBN: 9781922696311 (paperback)

Ford Street website: www.fordstreetpublishing.com

Cover design and map: Matt Lin © Ford Street Publishing

Printed in China by Tingleman Pty Ltd

To Naomi Woodward, Meredith Costain,
and others who helped polish this story — PC

Chapter One

It's funny the things you think about in times of peril. For instance, when a two-hundred-pound wild boar is charging at you. Winston was wondering why he couldn't just go to the market and purchase a leg of ham. He clutched his nine-foot boar spear with all his might. He didn't fancy his chances against a pair of tusks sharp enough to shave with.

The boars that lived in the ruins of the ancient city of Kalderial had recently developed a taste for human flesh, so Winston was using himself as bait. It had seemed a good idea at the time, proving that silly thoughts enter your mind even when not in times of peril.

At the very last moment the boar dodged to the right of the spearhead, then batted it aside with its snout. Winston dropped the spear, leapt straight up, and caught the rope he had left dangling from the branch above him as a worst-case scenario escape route.

Yes, it had definitely met hunters before, and probably eaten them, Winston thought as the boar jumped about and squealed just below him, slashing at him with its tusks. Winston drew a sword that had been old when his grandfather was a baby. If he could annoy it enough it mightn't think he was worth the effort.

Winston slashed wildly at the enraged boar, but it dodged the sword's point with surprising skill. It had experience with evading edged weapons and was armed with a couple of impressively-edged weapons of its own. Winston's long, pale hair kept getting in his eyes, but he was holding the rope with one hand and his sword with the other, so tying it back wasn't an option. Nor was wiping the salty sweat from his eyes.

When Winston had set up his escape rope, he had tied one end around the trunk of a tree and tossed the other over an overhanging branch. Now the boar slashed at the rope tied to the trunk. With a jolt of alarm Winston realised this was no feral pig – rather one with as much cunning as a market rat. Winston knew what was going to happen next. It was one of those 'can-this-get-any-worse?' moments to which you know the depressing answer. The rope snapped. Winston fell. The sword wrenched out of his hand and he crashed down onto bristles and rock-hard muscles.

After a moment Winston realised that he was alive and lying on the ground, rather than bleeding to death and being eaten. He drew his knife and waved it at the boar. No reaction. It too was lying on the ground, and not in a happy place. Not even breathing. Then Winston saw the handle of his sword protruding from the boar's mouth. He nearly swooned with relief.

Despite the fact that the boar was dead, his problems weren't over. He still had to get its body back to where his master lived, half a mile away. It was quite difficult to extract the sword from the boar's mouth, but Winston had learned that always being armed was an excellent way to stay alive. Next, he fetched a wooden sled from behind a tree, dragged the boar onto it, then rigged a harness out of his rope and set off for home.

The ruins where he lived were so overgrown that they looked like a forest pretending to be a city, rather than what had once been the capital of the greatest empire on the continent of Dravinia. There had been no invading army or deadly plague; the river that powered the city's water mills and carried its cargo barges had burst its banks and changed course in an earthquake. Within five years mighty Kalderial was fast becoming abandoned, and in ten it was home to more wild beasts than people.

The boars and panthers now made it a dangerous place. Winston had boiled his white apprentice's robe in a pot with crushed vine leaves to turn it green, so that threats would be less likely to see him before he saw them. He could have dyed his hair green as well, but that would have meant putting his head in boiling water. It began to rain. Winston looked skyward. Rain? He chuckled. Rain was nothing compared with what he had just been through. But were he thinking straight, he would have known that taunting the gods was a very foolish thing to do. At that moment another boar appeared on the path ahead.

Winston's spear was tied to the sled with the first boar and the newcomer was already charging, so he only had time to draw his sword. Still harnessed to the sled, Winston couldn't dodge or even run. He slashed at the boar. It dodged his blade and lunged at him with its tusks front and centre. Winston flung himself flat to the ground – and lost his grip on his sword.

The boar lowered its head until one of its tusks was less than an inch from Winston's face. Winston knew without a doubt that it was pausing to gloat before it sliced his nose off. It was another moment before Winston calmly considered a pointless thought. Animals don't gloat, only humans do that. He wondered if someone had enchanted this monster to be brighter than it should be. Then again, this split-second thought reminded him that he knew of a forbidden spell that only worked on humans. At this stage of the encounter, anything was better than nothing.

In order to cast any sort of magic, a wizard has to trace a spell in the air with a fingertip. A glowing symbol then defines the spell, which hangs in the air like a hovering dragonfly until the user focuses the spell through it. Does the boar know what a signature spell is? Winston wondered. If it did, he was about to find out what happens after death.

Very slowly he traced a spell in the air, then closed his fingers around it. As Winston whispered a word of power to his fist, the boar glared at him with beady, bloodshot eyes and pressed a cold, hard and exceedingly sharp tusk against his cheek. It was now or never.

Winston slammed his enchanted fist between the boar's eyes – and it sank right through bristles, skin and bone until it reached its brain. Power surged through his arm as if he had been hit by lightning. The fact that the spell worked definitely meant someone had been using forbidden magic on these boars.

After what seemed like hours but was actually no more than a minute, the boar toppled sideways. Winston withdrew his hand from the animal's head. There was no wound on the boar, and although he had drained the life energy directly from its brain, there was no blood on Winston's fingers.

Winston sat back, exhausted. He pondered the fact that his master, the venerable Faramond Erris, was going to be angry if he learnt that his apprentice had killed this thing using magic.

Ignoring the pounding rain, he got up, hauled the second body onto the sled, and set off, dragging four hundred pounds of dead boar behind him.

Hunched over, he trudged along the muddy path. He supposed that he'd had worse days, but right then he couldn't remember one of them.

For Winston, home was a palace. True, it was a palace in a city abandoned two thousand years earlier, but it was still a palace. After the roofs decayed and collapsed, the palace garden had spread inside, and quite a lush patch of flowers and vegetables was now growing over the rubble on the throne room floor. The wizard Faramond Erris had cleared the vines, rubble and remains of the throne away from the stone platform where emperors had once reigned, then gathered some bricks and thatch, cut saplings, and built a hut.

Here Winston lived with Faramond. Winston had been the wizard's apprentice for a year and a half, and was now fourteen. It was Winston's looks that put him on the road to a career in magic. His hair was so pale it was almost white, and his eyes were bright green, so he had *looked* magical before he even learned his first spell. His mother was a herbalist and healer, and by the age of twelve he'd learned enough to treat most of her patients. His father was superstitious, however, and having a boy in the house who looked like an elf without the pointed ears made him uneasy.

A month before Winston turned thirteen, his father's nerve cracked. Looking like an elf was bad enough, but his son was about to become a thirteen-year-old, and that was sure to mean bad luck. They made the short journey to the ruins of Kalderial, where Winston was indentured to Faramond, a member of the Countercasts' Guild of Wizards.

It was not a happy match for either of them because Winston had the worst possible trait when it came to being an apprentice: he was a lot cleverer than his master.

Faramond was still asleep as Winston sewed up the gash in his cheek using a polished copper tray as a mirror. Back in one piece, and very pleased with himself for not fainting from the pain, he turned his attention to the fireplace.

He sighed wearily. All of his life he had dreamed of rescuing a princess from a dragon, marrying her, and living in a palace. Now he *was* living in a palace, but it was not the palace of his dreams.

Winston struck sparks into the tinder, but although some smoke curled up, no flames appeared. The scent of the smoke reached Faramond, who struggled free of the pile of rugs, furs and blankets he slept under. Like a bear risen from hibernation, he stood, stretched, belched, then pulled his faded and grubby red and gold robes over his nightshirt.

Faramond shambled over to where Winston was still trying to start a fire with damp tinder. The wizard was bald and had grown a long beard to make up for his lack of hair, and to command respect. Winston felt like telling him that it just made his head look like it was upside down, but he was smart enough to keep that opinion to himself.

'What? No breakfast on the boil?' the wizard exclaimed. He scratched away several fleas that were eating on his bulging stomach.

'Sorry, Master, the tinder is damp,' replied Winston.

Faramond speared him with a scowl. 'But you're trying to start the fire with a *tinder* box.'

'Yes, Master, I always start fires that way.'

'Just use the igniting spell, boy, and be done with it!'

'But Master, I don't have your reserves of weight. It will leave me too weak to do my other chores.'

'It's a cold, wet morning and I'm hungry. Just use the confounded spell!'

Winston winced at the wizard's ire. He dutifully traced a faintly glowing spell in the air, closed his fist over it, then pointed at the pile of damp kindling and said, '*Igienisen.*'

Life force can be converted into magical energies, and these power sources can be drawn upon to do useful things, like supplying heat to light fires. Unfortunately, Winston had forgotten he'd killed one of the boars by draining its life force into himself. The energies of the large and powerful boar flashed from Winston's extended finger and reached the fireplace, converting all the energy stored in the tinder and firewood into heat. If this energy had been liberated over three or four hours it would have boiled the stew for Faramond's breakfast, warmed the hut, and dried Winston's rain-soaked clothes. The problem was that the wood converted to heat in something less than a millionth of a second.

The explosion blew the fireplace apart, threw Faramond back across the room and into the nest of furs and blankets that he called his bed, and flung Winston out through the door. The door had been closed.

Some minutes later, Faramond glared as his apprentice gathered up what was left of the door to use as firewood, yet the wizard was more than a little frightened. Winston was already more powerful than him, but Faramond dared not tell him that. His thin, pale-haired apprentice might start demanding better food, a new robe, a proper bed, magical training – perhaps even money.

'Stupid boy, has nobody ever taught you control?' muttered Faramond when Winston brought the wood inside.

Winston squirmed. Faramond was negligent in such matters as teaching. 'No, Master.'

'Well, go outside and practise controlling that spell.'

'It's raining, Master.'

Faramond smiled fiendishly. 'Good! That's your punishment for being such a careless wretch!'

Winston walked toward the hole in the wall that had once been the door.

'Where do you think you're going?' shouted Faramond.

'You told me to—'

'Clean up in here first and start a fire. Where's my pot of breakfast stew?'

Winston pointed to a pot-sized hole in the roof. Giving up on the idea of a hot breakfast, Faramond took a leg of smoked ham from the pantry.

'Well, what did you catch this morning?' he asked between mouthfuls.

'The two wild boars on the sled outside, Master.'

'Ah, now they should roast up wonderfully! Last week I cast a spell on the local pigs to make them more intelligent about what they eat. It should have improved their flavour somewhat.'

'You could've warned me, Master.'

'*Warned* you? About what?'

'They also fight more intelligently.'

Winston pointed to the stitched-up slash on his right cheek.

Faramond smirked. 'Had a few problems with the porkers, then?'

Winston swallowed. 'They nearly killed me, Master.'

'Well, if you can't match wits with a pig then you shouldn't be my apprentice.'

Thousands of years living free had transformed the wild pigs of Kalderial from friendly, grunting mounds of bacon on legs that would do anything for a bucket of swill into red-eyed terrors with tusks like grubby cutlasses. Now Faramond had made them intelligent.

'You should be grateful,' the wizard continued, suddenly worried that he might have pushed Winston too far. 'How many other boys live in a palace?'

'It's been a ruin for two thousand years, Master.'

'It's *still* a palace,' said Faramond, slapping his apprentice across the ear for answering back.

———◆———

Faramond practised the Countercast style of magic. He could cast any type of spell as long as he sacrificed something to balance it. Countercast wizards ate a great deal and used body fat to fuel their spells. Winston had been thin to begin with, even though his mother had fed him a lot more than he was happy about. Practising simple spells had made him even leaner, but then he learned to sacrifice things like sleep or strength instead. It was this that led to his interest in a very ancient spell, and his early experiments had shown a lot of promise. It seemed like a good idea not to tell Faramond anything about this, but Winston's experiments were starting to catch up with him. The explosion in the fireplace might have been clumsiness, but there was something else in the hut that would be a lot harder to explain away.

'Did the carrier bats bring any messages last night?' asked Faramond.

This spells trouble, Winston thought as he took

a tiny, sealed scroll from his coin purse. He didn't need to read it to know that.

The apprentice bowed, then handed his master a tray with the scroll on it. Faramond examined the tiny blob of wax that sealed the little scroll, then cracked it. The colour drained from his face as he read.

'We have been summoned to appear before the Guild Elders, and *your* behaviour is to be investigated!' exclaimed the wizard in alarm, dropping the ham bone that he had been gnawing. 'What have you been up to?'

'Nothing,' said Winston automatically.

'The Guild Elders don't send out summonses because members have done nothing, you silly boy.'

Winston hesitated. 'Er, nothing much?'

'How do the Guild Elders even know you exist?'

'I gave a demonstration at the Young Magical Apprentices Conference in Haldan last month.'

Faramond waved the little scroll at Winston.

'Idiot boy! This is from the Guild Elders! They're angry. Precisely what did you do?' Faramond seemed to swoon for a moment.

'A bit of that. A bit of this.'

Winston's vagueness made Faramond's eyes squint.

Winston waved his hands, seemingly hoping that words would magically come to him. 'Just some simple healing charms and fire castings.'

'What *else*?'

'I . . . balanced the spells by using the energy of other apprentices.'

'*What?*' shrieked Faramond. 'That violates the very foundation of our guild. Countercast wizards must store up their own weight to cast spells! You can't go around willy-nilly stealing from your peers! It's – it's . . . unethical.' Faramond spread his arms wide, showing that he had vast reserves of body fat to power whatever magic he needed to perform. 'You don't think I like eating everything within eyesight, do you?!'

Winston knew a trick question when he heard it. Faramond's glaring beady eyes added weight to this. He slumped, momentarily at a loss. 'I don't like to overindulge,' said Winston.

'Why? Eating is one of life's greatest pleasures. Well, so long as you don't get carried away, of course.'

'Most Countercast wizards die from heart attacks,' Winston said.

'So? Lots of people die from heart attacks.'

'Countercast wizards die much younger. Mistress Aldar of the Healers' Sisterhood has dissected a dozen wizards from our guild. She said the arteries of Pantonic the Flatulent were clogged with—'

'Enough! That sort of talk will get you staked out in the desert with fire ants crawling up your nostrils and eating your brain, if they can find any brain to . . . Wait a moment. What's this conference you keep blathering about?'

'Well, some of us apprentices met in the Haldan market last month. We just happened to be there at the same time, buying provisions for our masters. There were fifteen of us and we decided to have a conference. We also organised ourselves into the Young Magical Apprentices Union. They elected me union representative, and I plan to petition the Guild Elders for things like a one-hundred-and-twenty-hour week—'

'A one-hundred-and-twenty-hour week? I'll give you a one-hundred-and-twenty-hour *day*! What else?'

'Annual conference leave, beds, two hours of study time per day, wages of one shilling per month—'

'*Wages!*' shrieked Faramond. 'This is beyond bearing. It's the end of wizardry as we know it! Find the donkey and pack for a journey. With luck the elders will only want you drowned in bat bile, and I'll be free to seek a less demanding apprentice.'

Although the rain had stopped by now, the overgrown ruins of the abandoned city were thoroughly soaked. Water dripped from wet trees and mud squelched underfoot as Winston set off to fetch the donkey. He carried his boar spear in case there were any boars nearby who were feeling cranky about him killing two of their kindred.

The donkey was asleep in a shelter that Winston had rigged up for him, and was quite dry – unlike the drenched apprentice. He was leading the animal across a small clearing fringed with brambles when he spied what seemed to be a knight wearing expensive-looking plate armour and carrying a lance.

'You there, the boy in the green dress!' the stranger called. 'I'm looking for a dragon.'

This was the sort of opening remark that was meant to tell Winston he was speaking with a member of the nobility, and that he had better show some respect or he'd be sorry. The knight wasn't to know that Winston was in the third hour of a very bad morning. Worse, he was fourteen, and feeling the very first stirrings of teenage rebellion.

Winston decided that he'd had enough that morning. That clown's voice hasn't yet broken, so he's probably younger than me, he mused. The knight was either a pretend knight or an apprentice with no more training than him. If he could beat magically intelligent boars, he could beat an untrained boy on a nag. Furthermore, he was about to leave an overgrown ruin, go on a long journey, be put on trial, and probably get executed. Why not share the misery around?

'I'm a wizard's apprentice, and this is a *robe*,' he replied. 'Now be off with you before my temper gets the better of me.'

'Show some respect or I'll ride you down and trample you into the mud,' the horseman declared.

Winston counted to ten. 'If you're looking for dragons, try Summer Gate.' He walked on, deliberately leaving before being told to be on *his* way. Insulted, the knight spurred his horse and charged at Winston.

The nine-foot boar spear should have been a hint that the almost skeletally thin, pale youth had been catching and killing his master's breakfast, lunch and dinner on a regular basis, and that his master liked pork from boars with huge tusks and serious attitude problems.

Boar spears have an iron crossbar eighteen inches from the spearhead, because an impaled boar is quite capable of charging the length of a spear, scoring a double kill on the hunter. As the knight bore down on Winston, he released the donkey and swung his spear up with the skill that comes from over a hundred encounters with angry free-range pork. He caught the rider under the arm with the crossbar, sidestepped the charging horse, and dropped the end of the spear into the ground.

The armoured youth was lifted right out of his saddle and pitched into a thicket of brambles. The donkey bolted. The horse decided that his services were not required for the moment and began to graze on the lush grass. For a moment Winston watched the armoured limbs thrashing about amid the tangles of thorny branches, then set off after his donkey. What a depressingly stupid knight, he thought, shaking his head.

It was noon by the time Winston managed to catch the donkey, return to the palace, and pack the saddlebags and his backpack.

He decided it best to keep quiet when Faramond cursed him for taking his time.

Winston and Faramond set off for Summer Gate with the wizard uneasily straddling the donkey. Winston cheered up, preferring being on the road to life in the ruins of Kalderial. Now he was actually going somewhere, and dinner wasn't trying to eat him. True, he was hauling a sled along the muddy path with two heavy boars tied to it, but he reminded himself he was leaving Kalderial, probably forever – not that 'forever' was likely to be very long.

By contrast, Faramond was in a very bad mood.

'In all my years, boy, no apprentice of mine has ever disgraced me so,' he grumbled. 'Follow in my footsteps and you can gain the skills to work for kings and emperors. Instead, you read! You must have a secret stash of ancient books somewhere. When I find it I'll burn it to ashes. What was your talk about, anyway?'

Winston cleared his throat. 'It was about the Lost Spell of Yoal, Master.'

'It must have been such a pile of rubbish that nobody took it seriously until it was too late. Show it to me.'

Winston unslung his backpack, and unpacked the speech he had given at the conference. He handed it to Faramond, along with a small metal jug. The wizard looked at the inscription engraved on the side.

'I based it on those words,' said Winston.

'Where did you get this?' demanded Faramond.

'In the market at Loseros.'

'The jug dates from when this city had people in it.' His eyes narrowed. 'I have a bad feeling about this.'

'But Master, why?'

'Because some lost things are lost for very good reasons.'

Faramond liked a quiet life. He wanted the lost spell to be gone forever. It was said to bind wizards together into something with the powers to defeat even dragons. This worried him because such a spell was of interest to dragons as well as the Guild Elders. Attracting dragons was like hauling a shark into a fishing boat: they were bad company at close quarters and didn't listen to excuses.

Although Faramond would have preferred the lost spell to stay lost, Winston had given a talk on it, and other wizards' apprentices had made notes and showed them to their masters. He had to think of some convincing explanation, preferably one that put all the blame on Winston.

He read through the speech that Winston had given as they moved on. Being short, it didn't take long to read.

'It's all a myth from start to finish, or I'm no wizard,' concluded Faramond. 'You can't even start a fire – and speaking of starting fires, how did you store up so much power?'

'Master?'

'The energies that caused that explosion in my fireplace! Even I couldn't have done that.'

Winston feigned surprise. It was inevitable the cagey old coot would ask *that* question.

'I . . . was fighting a boar.'

'And?'

'And it seemed too intelligent to be a natural boar, so I thought it might be possessed by a human spirit. I was fighting for my life, Master. It was it or me.'

'What did you do?' probed Faramond.

'I cast a spell based on my talk.'

Faramond grew wide-eyed with alarm, his normally ruddy face the colour of chalk. 'Winston, exactly how did you kill the pig?' he asked, his voice barely more than a whisper.

'I was pinned down. You can see the slash I got on my right cheek from its tusk. I . . . enchanted my hand, reached into its head and drew out its life force.'

'You *what?*' shrieked the wizard.

'I—'

'*Stupid* boy! Casting human intelligence on animals draws the death penalty! If the Guild Elders ever find out that I enhanced those pigs . . .'

Faramond's voice trailed off, realising he was in as much trouble as Winston. He rode in silence for a few minutes, thinking through his options, then concluded that he only had one: a truce.

'Look, perhaps we had better stick together when we testify to the Guild Elders,' he conceded. 'If you don't mention that the pigs of Kalderial were brighter than they should have been, I shall testify that you are merely a little too diligent, and that you got ahead of me with your studies. They might even take you off my hands and apprentice you to someone better suited to managing your talents.'

'Whatever you say, Master.'

Although he didn't show it, Winston was

elated. Not only would Faramond be forced to help him, his testimony might get him a better master. He was tempted to smile, but he knew that Faramond would always get bad-tempered when he seemed happy. The wizard said that smiling people were actually concealing lies, secrets and conspiracies.

Again, Faramond stared at the ancient inscription on the jug. He wouldn't admit it, but the words unsettled him.

'The words seem to leap out at you, don't they?' he said.

'Yes, Master. That's why they caught my interest.'

Faramond now glared at the jug as if it had insulted him. The words seemed to make him want to say them. He mouthed the text silently, and found himself longing to speak the lines aloud:

Why is lost, but shall be found,

See to my skip above the ground.

Faramond tore his eyes away.

'Today we give this to the dragon Griffid as

price of passage, along with the two boars,' he decided.

'But Master—'

'Silence! I want to be rid of this jug, clown! Once it's safely in the dragon's hoard the Guild Elders cannot blame me for not reporting it to them. If the spell can be lost, the jug can be too. You found it in a market, you say?'

'Yes, when we were in Loseros last year. It cost me two copper shots. The vendor was anxious to get rid of it. He said it talked to him in his dreams. It told him of the Blackstone Tower.'

'So why did you buy such a vessel? Surely you could sense trouble?'

'The Blackstone Tower is the world's most famous place of magical power. I was intrigued.'

'Winston, here is some advice that might keep you alive long enough to reach your fifteenth birthday. When you encounter something strange and powerful that intrigues you, the best thing to do is circle around it very quietly, then run like the wind itself. The Lost Spell of Yoal is not just some conjuring trick allowing wizards to borrow energy from each other. It's said to be the key to Blackstone Tower.'

'Who said that?' asked Winston.

'Wizards. Important wizards. Why do you want to know?'

'I have questions.'

'Well, I'm an important wizard. Ask me.'

'How can the spell do more than one trick?'

'Trick? Trick?' cried Faramond. 'The spell does not do tricks, it performs mighty enchantments.'

'But—'

'Winston, the spell is like a battleaxe. You can use it to fight an enemy, or you can chop firewood with it.'

'But all I'd like to do is get into the Tower.'

'And do what?'

Winston shrugged. 'Just . . . look around. See what all the fuss is about.'

'Idiot boy! Blackstone Tower is surrounded by the most powerful magic imaginable. Some of our Countercast wizards have flung the best of their enchantments against it without even scratching the door. It withered them from very large and powerful men like me to walking skeletons wearing robes.'

'But Master—'

'Silence! Say, just say, that you break into the Tower. What do you think will be your reward?'

'I've never thought about rewards.'

'The elders will hate you for it! Mark my words, they don't like apprentices a quarter their age doing what they can't.'

Winston thought through what the wizard had said – and what he had not. The jug had given Winston dreams as well, but not Faramond. Why? The truth was that Faramond's mind was closed to new ideas, and it was the same for the elders.

For all of his life people had been shouting at him that they were older and wiser, so he should do things their way. His mother always knew best about herbs, and his grandmother beat him with her walking stick if he tried his own improvements on her healing spells. His father was a market constable and fancied himself a warrior, so whatever Winston did with a spear, sword or quarterstaff was bound to be wrong. Faramond shouted at him no matter *what* he did.

Winston had not yet learned that 'older' usually meant more foolish rather than wiser, but no older person was going to admit it. Young people had to discover that for themselves, and they usually did so around the age of fourteen. He didn't realise it, but he was already a more dangerous fighter than his father, had discovered more exotic herbs in the ruins of Kalderial than his mother had ever heard of, and could cast spells that would make his grandmother run screaming – or at least hobble away fairly rapidly. Unlike Faramond, he liked to read rather than eat, so he had overtaken the wizard in many areas of scholarship.

Until now, Winston had learned to stay out of trouble by doing what he was told when people were watching, being polite, pretending to be stupid, and performing his experiments with spell casting in secret. All that would have to change if he wanted to stay alive long enough to turn fifteen.

Some miles away, the armoured warrior that Winston had pitched into the brambles finally struggled free of the grasping, thorny branches, removed the brightly polished helmet, and flung it to the grass. Not only was the warrior's face that of someone not yet needing to shave, it was a face that would never need shaving at all.

Larissa de Green, the daughter of Hugo de Green, Captain of the Riversend Lancers, looked around for her adversary. Apart from her horse, she was alone.

'I'll get you for that!' she screamed at the overgrown buildings of the abandoned city.

Her horse looked up, decided that the words weren't for him, and returned to cropping the grass. Quite a few ants had found their way into Larissa's armour in the hours it had taken to struggle free of the brambles. The ants were also beneath her quilted padding, tunic and trousers. Just in case her lower-class but annoyingly skilled opponent was watching from behind cover, Larissa set up her tent and crawled inside to strip off completely and purge the ants from her clothing.

Heroes in legends get to kill a thousand enemy warriors, but I kill a thousand ants, she thought as she worked. How humiliating. Almost as humiliating as being defeated in my first genuine clash of arms by a peasant in a dress.

It took another hour to get dressed again, pack

her tent, then struggle back into her armour without the help of a squire. It was quite late in the day by now, and she didn't fancy the idea of camping out in the ruins after her disastrous encounter with one of the locals.

Larissa studied a map. She had come in through Summer Gate without so much as a whiff of a dragon. According to the map, there was an inn outside the walls, not far from Winter Gate. Inns had stables and stables had stable hands who could help with getting armour on and off. They served hot meals and had beds. It would take thirty or forty days to search the ruins, using the inn as a base. She had enough silver for that. It seemed a sensible plan.

Larissa was four years older than Winston, and because she'd spent her life making up for not being a son by training to be a knight, she was strong, skilled and formidable when it came to jousting, fencing and archery. On the other hand, her life had never once been in danger. She didn't yet know the horror of facing death. For Winston, it was just part of shopping for food that was trying to kill him.

Chapter Two

Griffid was a large dragon who lived beside the Summer Gate of the old city wall. Many centuries earlier he'd been expelled from the island of Dracondas by the other dragons that lived there. Nobody was sure why, but the most popular theory was that he was as lazy as Faramond and they wanted him out of sight. He now spent nearly all his time asleep, and vines had actually grown over him since his last meal. That was how Larissa had missed him as she rode into the city.

The city's gates and palace marked the beginning of summer and winter. The palace was at the centre of the city, and the day that the setting sun was visible at the palace through Summer Gate marked the beginning of summer. The first day of winter was marked when those in the palace could see the setting sun through

Winter Gate, in the southwest of the city walls. Since the city had been abandoned, the trees overgrowing the place got in the way, of course.

Winter Gate was unguarded, but leaving through it would have added five miles to the journey and Faramond didn't like travelling. Winston knew which pile of vines, ivy and bushes concealed Griffid, so while Faramond sat watching on the donkey, the youth walked up to a rocky outcrop and politely tapped at it with his spear. Something grunted. Winston tapped again.

Go away, muttered a deep voice in Winston's mind.

'I'm a wizard and this is my magical staff.'

You're an apprentice, that's a spear, and it's not magical. If you are here to look at your books, just do so.

Winston glanced back to Faramond, but the wizard was too far away for the dragon's thought speech to reach his mind.

'I'm here to pay price of passage,' said Winston. 'I have two fresh boars and a very nice jug.'

Winston held up the jug. Slowly, grudgingly, an enormous head rose, tearing free from the vines that had grown over it during the months past.

The rocky outcrop that Winston had tapped was one of its horns.

Griffid looked old even though he was fairly young for a dragon. His black and grey hide was blotched by lichen, and the teeth that had once crunched through the expensive armour of famous knights were now yellow because he didn't eat enough wood. His silver wings and immense body remained buried under the vines.

Once he realised it was safe to do so, Faramond spurred his donkey forward. 'Morning!' he called cheerfully.

More vines and ivy tore away as Griffid turned to look at the wizard.

Faramond. You look delicious.

'That's not funny!' Faramond squeaked.

Why did your boy wake me?

'We're passing, we have to pay you tribute,' said Winston, holding up the jug again.

You could have just added it to my hoard without waking me. Morach would have told me.

A large black bird cawed at Winston from one of the dragon's spines still visible above the vines.

'The crow is now your clerk?'

Raven. Remember, she was a mighty sorceress until she

lost a magical duel. Just deal with her the next time you come past. Don't bother waking me.

'*Caw!*' said Morach.

Winston decided it would be best to stay on the right side of Morach. He fished in his ragged sleeve for a scrap of bacon gristle that he had saved to chew on for lunch, and held it up. The raven launched herself at him, pecked his finger and ignored the offering. He swatted her away and the bacon scrap fell at his feet. Something small and furry darted between his legs, snatched it up and vanished among the leaves.

She's used to better fare than that, said Griffid.

For a third time, Winston held up the metal jug for Griffid's inspection, taking care to keep his hand over the inscription.

'Will this and the two boars do for payment of passage?' he asked.

Yes, yes, add it to the hoard. You know the way.

Griffid gulped down the two boars, and most of Winston's sled – the latter being purely for the sake of his teeth, of course.

The dragon kept his hoard in the ruins of what had once been a watchtower beside the city gates. The gates had long ago been looted for firewood, and some forgotten prince had salvaged part of the tower to build a castle, but the base was still round, solid and formidable. Winston climbed a wooden ladder propped against the side.

'Worth at least four sovereigns,' called Faramond, who steadfastly refused to go any closer. 'The jug, that is.'

Five copper shots, replied Griffid. *I have ninety-eight such jugs, but every one is much finer. The best of them was fashioned by the great silversmith Dinchelar. That one dates back to the Wizard Wars when the old Brotherhood of Enchanters fought back the undead warriors of Golmordus. It was payment for my part in the Last Battle of Ootbacken.*

'Were you not hatched two years *after* the battle?' called Winston before he could stop himself.

Chronicler's error, muttered Griffid. *Leave it with the other jugs, don't just throw it anywhere. Morach nags at me if I don't keep a tidy hoard.*

Winston climbed over the edge of the tower into Griffid's hoard. Some of it was just kitchen utensils that weren't made from precious metals. But there was a huge mound silver coins, and many gold coins sprinkled amongst them. He put the jug down beside half a dozen others.

'I thought you said you have ninety-eight jugs,' called Winston. 'I count six.'

Some hero on a quest must have stolen the others.

Winston made his way across to a battered wooden chest and opened the lid. Inside were old leather-bound books. Winston examined them. None had been taken, and the rain had not penetrated the lid. His notes were still there as well. Satisfied that his secret library was still secret and undamaged, he climbed out of the hoard and back down the ladder.

Tribute accepted, now leave me alone, Griffid muttered.

'Did you know there's a knight looking for you?' said Winston.

A knight? Don't like knights. All that trouble to get them out of their armour, and half an hour later you could do with another.

'He must have ridden right past without seeing you.'

Ridden? Now horses are a different matter, although the saddles can be a bit chewy.

The donkey appeared to understand the dragon's words. He reared, throwing Faramond off, along with the saddlebags, then bolted.

'You would have to say that!' shouted Faramond. 'We'll never catch him now.'

So he's feral, and without an owner? said Griffid. *Excellent.*

With that the dragon reared up, shook the accumulation of vines from his body and spread his wings. The downdraft blew Winston off the ladder as the creature launched himself into the air and flew away in pursuit of the donkey.

'It was your fault that the donkey got eaten,' said Faramond as they passed through the gap in the old city wall that had once been a magnificent gate.

Faramond was now riding a large feral pig. Winston had tracked it down, then offered himself to it as bait. When it charged him, it ran straight into the snare rigged up in what had once been an exclusive street in the city. Faramond then cast a hypnosis spell to convince it that it was a donkey, and didn't eat humans.

'Lost half the afternoon catching this thing,' the wizard grumbled. 'And it's undignified. Whoever heard of a famous wizard riding breakfast? Why did you tell the dragon about that knight and raise the matter of eating horses?'

'I didn't know the donkey understood human speech, Master.'

'I cast a very minor spell on him this morning, so that I could command him more easily as I rode.'

'You could've told me.'

'I'm your master, I don't have to tell you anything.'

'Does the boar understand human speech?'

'I'm not making *that* mistake again.'

After another few miles, the forest covering Kalderial gave way to open pasture, but the boundary between pasture and forest held another threat.

The man who stepped out onto the strip of mud that passed for the road was holding a crossbow. This was meant to tell Winston and Faramond that he was seriously dangerous. There was a sharp snap from the bushes to the left, and a crossbow bolt half-buried itself in the mud at Winston's feet. This was meant to tell Winston that the man in front of him was not alone. He dropped his boar spear and raised his hands.

'Do nothing rash, and no harm will happen, except to your purses,' declared the man on the road.

'Understood, sir,' said Winston.

'I'll have you know I'm a very senior and powerful wizard, and you are in a lot of trouble!' declared Faramond, who had been gnawing on a ham bone.

A crossbow bolt from the bushes took the ham bone out of Faramond's grasp. He raised his hands and shut his mouth.

Politely, Winston said, 'May I lower my hands and untie my purse, sir?'

'I insist,' said the highwayman.

They were in bright sunlight, so the highwayman couldn't see the glowing spell that Winston's fingers traced as he untied his purse. He closed the fingers of his right hand over the spell as he tossed the purse to the highwayman with his left. Winston coughed. The cough became a coughing fit, and he innocently put his right fist to his mouth and whispered '*Risium.*'

The highwayman began to snigger, pointing at

Faramond astride a boar and wearing grubby red and gold robes. The sniggering became laughter. Behind Winston, Faramond was laughing too, and Winston laughed as well, so as not to seem suspicious. The highwayman fell to his knees in the mud, dropping his crossbow, then rolled about kicking his legs in the air, shrieking hysterically.

At this point another brigand emerged from the bushes, crossbow at the ready, to see what was so funny. As he approached Faramond he suddenly clapped a hand over his mouth, dropped his crossbow and collapsed, helpless with mirth. Now two more men broke cover, both with swords drawn. Faramond toppled from the boar, his hands still held high. The swordsmen approached, and burst out laughing before they reached the edge of Winston's spell. Once they had advanced a little closer their fate was sealed.

Winston lowered his hands, then checked the nearby bushes, but there were no more brigands in the gang. Next, he gathered up their weapons and purses. The crossbows and swords he tied across the saddlebags; the purses vanished under his robe. Faramond shrieked with laughter as Winston tied the four brigands together and left them in the middle of the road for the next traveller to liberate – or ignore. It proved impossible to get the wizard astride the boar again, so Winston finally gave up and tied him across its back.

'Anyone with an ounce of willpower could've resisted that casting,' muttered Winston as he set off again, leading the boar and weak from the effort of casting the spell. 'I wonder if it's possible to draw on Faramond's energies to restore myself? No, that's icky; it'd be too much like being a cannibal.'

By sunset they had reached a hamlet with an inn. A snap of Winston's fingers broke the spell, but by now Faramond had been laughing for so long that his cries of outrage were little more than peevish wheezes. Winston paid the innkeeper to prepare a bath. He then visited the local blacksmith's shop, where he sold the two crossbows and four swords. Faramond was in the bath eating dinner when the youth returned to the inn.

'Idiot boy!' he called hoarsely. 'I've never been

so humiliated in all my life! Where have you been?'

'Selling the brigands' weapons, Master.'

'How much did you get?'

'Two hundred silver—'

'Give them here! Why didn't you break the spell as soon as you had the brigands tied up?'

Winston put a hand to his mouth and gasped. 'Oh, Master, you're right! How stupid of me. As you always say, I have so much to learn.'

Faramond mumbled something indecipherable and struggled out of the bath. Wrapped in a towel and blanket he made his way to the taproom where he ordered ale and three more pies. Winston settled down for the night in a pile of hay in the stables. Using his last reserves of stolen energies, he traced a spell in the air, closed a fist over the glowing symbol, and opened his fingers to reveal a pinhead of bright light in the palm of his hand.

After counting the seventeen silver shillings he had stolen from the brigands, Winston propped a book from his secret stash against his knees, took a chunk of Faramond's smoked ham from his robes, and settled down for the evening. Life is pretty grim when sleeping on straw in a stable and dining on stolen food is a luxury, he thought. In the distance Faramond shouted that there was half a mouse in one of the pies. On the other hand, it could be worse.

The fishing port where Winston had been born was twenty-five miles further down the road, and they reached it late the following afternoon. By then Faramond was redefining the meaning of the term *ugly mood*, due to ten hours of other travellers, wayfarer constables, shepherds and farm labourers laughing at the sight of a wizard in a mud-splattered but otherwise magnificent red and gold robe astride a pig.

The port's name was Loseros, which meant *lost port* in some ancient language. The name might have been a joke in the distant past, but it had stuck, even though various town councils had tried to modernise the name. This was partly because much of the town had been lost beneath the sea.

'Might I suggest that you dismount before we enter Loseros, Master?' said Winston, as respectfully as he could manage.

'Whatever for?'

'So you will not have the entire town laughing at you.'

'Ah yes, good point.'

The prospect of being somewhere with good food softened Faramond's mood, and although he had to walk the last half mile, he cheered up a lot.

'I grew up here, boy,' the wizard mused. 'Don't be surprised. My beginnings were just as humble as yours. When I was younger the sea was a five-minute stroll from the market plaza. Now it moves a foot or so inland every year, and the townsfolk spend more time rebuilding their houses further west than they do fishing. Some say that the beautiful young countess who once ruled the province drowned when her ship was caught in a storm, so the town is drowning itself in sorrow. More enlightened folk say that an enormous slumbering dragon is slowly rolling in its sleep beneath the ground, causing the coast to sink.'

'I noticed that there are three or four small earth tremors every year, Master,' said Winston.

'Each time there was a tremor I measured the water level on the side of the light tower at high tide, and it always rose an inch or so.'

'So what?' scoffed Faramond. 'Earth tremors are caused by underground dragons rolling in their sleep.'

'Has anyone ever seen one?'

'Of course not, they're under the ground.'

Winston pointed to a volcano on an island a few miles out to sea.

'Molten rocks flow out of that volcano, Master. I think that leaves space underneath, so the ground drops.'

'Stupid boy! That volcano is the dragon's mouth.'

Winston sighed inwardly. For a year and a half, he'd been studying to be a wizard. All he had learned from Faramond was that wizards eat a lot and they didn't like new ideas. Most of the magic he knew he'd taught himself. This is a seriously depressing way to learn a trade, he thought.

They passed through the gates of Loseros. Twice. The defensive wall was being rebuilt a hundred yards further inland. The old market had moved too, but it was only made up of tents, vendors' carts and merchants' wagons, so it was a lot more portable. Merchants of every kind, self-declared wizards, healer witches, journeymen, mercenaries, traders, trappers, scribes and thieves of every description made a living there. Every so often someone would suggest that Loseros be moved a few miles north, where the coast was not subsiding, but it never happened. The real estate priests said the earth dragon would be offended if they moved, so life went on as before.

The air reeked of dung, cooking fat, herbs, tanneries, dyeing vats, fish, and above all, unwashed humans. After so much time spent in the pure air of Kalderial's ruins and on the open road, this came as quite a shock to both the wizard and his apprentice.

'I don't remember it being such a stinking mess when I was a boy,' called Faramond above the din of hawkers shouting about their wares, haggling customers, shrieks of fishwives, rumbling wagons, neighing horses, snorting pigs, barking dogs and occasional cries of 'Stop, thief!'.

'It all looks and smells pretty normal to me,' replied Winston.

They stopped at a pie stall, where Faramond

bought one to last him until dinner. Winston tethered the boar to a horse rail, removed the saddlebags, and sat on them.

'Oi, you can't tie your pig 'ere! This be a horse rail!' called a market clerk.

Winston untethered the boar and held the reins in his hand. Presently, Faramond returned, pushed Winston off the saddlebags and sat down. After eating most of the pie, he tossed the crust to Winston. Winston waited until Faramond looked away, then tossed it to the boar.

'Master, I need to visit my parents to collect some things for the journey,' he said.

Faramond's reply was just a grunt, but he nodded, so Winston handed the reins to him. Faramond tied them to an ankle, leaned back against the wheel of a vendor's cart, belched contentedly, and closed his eyes. As Winston picked up his backpack, he had the feeling that he was being watched. Once clear of Faramond, he stopped, turning in time to see a gutter wizard approaching the boar. He waved his hand above it, tracing a spell and casting an enchantment to break what he thought was an obedience spell.

Two thousand years of evolution in the ruins

of Kalderial were liberated in an instant. The boar scrambled into motion, boring a path straight through the stalls, pushcarts, shoppers and merchants, and dragging Faramond behind him by the leg. A market constable tried to stop it by holding up his hand and shouting 'Halt!', then realised that a pair of tusks the size of boning knives backed up by four hundred pounds of raw bacon was bearing down on him at a gallop. He leapt aside.

Winston raced in the boar's wake and caught up when the animal stopped to smash an offal barrel and have dinner. He watched as a market constable shot the boar with a crossbow. A crowd of angry vendors gathered around the mortified Faramond.

Winston decided that this was a good time to quietly slip away and visit his parents. He soon arrived at a clay-brick cottage with a weatherworn sign showing a mortar and pestle, the sign of an apothecary. A canvas awning stretched above the shopfront, flapping restlessly, even though there was no breeze. The words *Molly Spellwyn* and *Herbs and Healing* were painted on it.

'Thief sail,' said a voice behind him. 'Best not

to take anything without paying or it will fly after you and wrap you up until the constables arrive.'

'I'm not a felon,' retorted Winston, turning to see that the speaker was driving a garbage wagon.

'Porrel!' he exclaimed. 'Good to see you, little sister.'

Winston's little sister was in fact bigger than he was, and quite a lot stronger. Beside her on the driver's seat was Fang, her terrier. They jumped down to the road together.

'Fang, my favourite hound,' said Winston, dropping to his knees and patting the dog. 'How has competition been lately?'

'Champion ratter of the Fish Market Tournament third month in a row,' said Porrel proudly. 'Two hundred and thirty rats killed in the time measured out by the official hourglass.'

There was a scream of recognition from within the shop.

'Winston!' Molly Spellwyn cried as she bustled out and buried him in a smothering embrace. 'It's been so many years since you visited!'

'I was here last month, Mother.'

'And you're so thin.'

'I do a lot of running.'

'And look at your tatty robes! Why aren't you a rich wizard by now?'

'I'm an apprentice, Mother. We don't get paid.'

'What? Even your useless sister gets thirty coppers a day driving the garbage wagon in the market. Why did you agree to an apprenticeship?'

'I didn't. Dad did.'

'What? Ah, yes. The fool wanted you out of the house before you turned thirteen.'

'Porrel is thirteen now. Does she still live here?'

'Aye,' said Porrel.

'Haven't you heard the news?' asked Molly.

'I've been away for a month.'

'Your father's passed. There was an accident.'

'Dead?' exclaimed Winston. 'That's terrible! How did it happen? Did he die fighting some gang of market thieves?'

'No, he was thrown out of the Jolly Barrel after one ale too many and hit his head on the gutter outside,' said Porrel. 'Jik Dredger parked his nightsoil wagon on top of him, thinkin' he was a pile of old rags. Just bad luck.'

'So, he sent me away in case I brought him bad luck, then died of bad luck without my help.'

'Have some respect,' said Molly.

Winston had never been close to his father, who had been foul-tempered when drunk and merely bad-tempered when sober.

'Molly? Who's there?'

An older replica of Winston's mother hobbled out of the shop, leaning on a cane. There was something strange about her teeth, and her hair didn't look quite right either.

'Gran?' exclaimed Winston.

'Winston! You're too thin and wearing rags,' she said, waving her walking stick at him. 'Why aren't you rich by now?'

'You have false teeth,' said Winston, taking care to stay out of range of her stick.

'What of it?'

'They're sharks' teeth.'

'Got 'em cheap at the fish market.'

'And a horsehair wig.'

'Keeps me old head warm.'

'I suppose you want dinner,' Molly Spellwyn interjected.

'No, no, my master and I are . . . just passing through,' said Winston, knowing that she would charge for the meal.

'Where are you going?' asked Molly.

'Important meeting of the elders of our guild.'

'The Guild?' snapped Molly. 'I despise 'em. No respect for hedgerow witches like me. What can those wizards do that I can't?'

'Eat enough for a week at one sitting,' said Gran Spellwyn. 'You just watch out for their High Sorceress Yolantha, Winston. She'll ensnare you m'boy.'

'Yes, Gran.' To avert further conversation, he gave Porrel his boar spear in return for their dead father's bow and arrows. The Countercasts' Guild Sanctum was in a desert, and he was unlikely to encounter any boars there, or return to Kalderial. He and Porrel set off for the Constables' Watchouse on the garbage wagon.

'Any word of big sister Stanni?' asked Winston.

'She's been promoted to Seaman Second Class on a coastal trader.'

'Seaman? But she's not a man.'

'At first, she was called Seagirl Stanni, then some of the sailors started calling her Seagull Stanni. After she sent five of them to the infirmary in as many days, the captain said she was to be called Seaman Stanni and he would hear no arguments. By then her knuckles were getting sore from hitting people, so she decided that Seaman Stanni was a good compromise. Her ship's in port at the moment, we could visit her before the tide turns.'

'I'd like that, but first I should check what happened to my master.'

Faramond was in the public stocks. He was bruised, battered and grubby from being towed along behind the boar, and his robes were now more ragged than Winston's. When Winston and Porrel arrived, market urchins were pelting him with rotten fruit and vegetables.

The desk constable said the boar's rampage had done five hundred silver shillings worth of damage, and that the saddlebags had apparently been stolen. Fortunately, the money for the journey had been in a purse tied to Faramond's belt. Unfortunately, the purse contained a handful of gold and silver to the value of precisely five hundred shillings.

Being the son of a market constable, Winston

got a sympathetic hearing when he asked for Faramond's release.

'We're going to the sanctum to have my apprenticeship reviewed,' he explained, stretching the truth but not quite lying. 'It would hurt my career if Faramond doesn't testify for me.'

'For Sergeant Grek's boy, I suppose I can set the miscreant free. Are you sure he's a wizard?'

'He's wearing wizard robes.'

'Could've stolen them, but I'll take your word for it,' said the desk clerk as he tossed a small cloth purse to Winston.

'Cleaver Jak the butcher paid fifteen shillings for the dead pig. Will that get you to the sanctum?'

'Could do. My thanks, sir.'

Faramond was released from the stocks, and after washing himself in a horse trough, he climbed onto the garbage wagon with Winston and Porrel and they set off for the docks.

'I suppose you expect thanks for setting me free,' muttered the wizard as the cart rumbled along.

'No, Master.'

'Insolent boy!' snapped Faramond.

When they reached the docks, Faramond went straight to a tavern and ordered a meal of poached eggs with rich golden yolks, thick herbed bacon, crisp potato fritters, slices of soft crusty stone bread and golden gooseberry pie served with corn syrup, whipped cream and custard sauce, and a platter of light fluffy cakes. Winston paid.

'Give me the rest of your money,' demanded Faramond between mouthfuls.

'I need it to pay for transport,' Winston replied. 'We already have to walk the sixty miles to Haldan, then we need to hire a sand cart to cross the hundred miles of desert to the sanctum.'

The prospect of a hundred-mile walk beat Faramond's plans to follow dinner with several more dinners.

'All right, all right! Just get out of my sight.'

Winston and Porrel left the tavern and returned to the garbage wagon.

'He likes his food, then?' said Porrel.

'He calls it wizard fuel,' replied Winston.

'Oi, I've got a sweetheart! Baker's son.'

'Good for you,' Winston said, nudging her with an elbow.

'I get all the fish pie I can eat. Got one in the cart, want half?'

Winston and Porrel set off along the wharf, sharing the pie and leaving Fang to guard the wagon.

'Scallan's a good cook,' said Porrel. 'Four years more and we're of an age to marry.'

'Wish I could marry. It would get me away from Faramond. He barely tolerates me.'

'Well, when I marry, I'll move out of home, have a bath and drive a beer wagon.'

'You'll always be popular, smelling of beer.'

There was a pause in the conversation, but Porrel knew her brother well enough to guess what he was thinking.

'You want to ask about Dad's funeral, don't you?'

'All right, how was the old wretch's funeral?'

'Cheap. Mum kept his body in a barrel of the spoilt ale until Stanni was in port. When she sailed a couple of days later, Dad was aboard, too.'

'Burial at sea?'

'Aye. It's cheap.'

They arrived at the *Salt Dragon*, where their older sister was helping prepare the little coaster to sail with the tide. She was seventeen, also taller than Winston, and broader across the shoulders. Her hands were black from the tar on the ropes.

'So, you're off to Haldan?' said Stanni brightly, hugging Winston until his ribs ached. 'So's the ship, want to come along? You can be in Haldan this time tomorrow – and travel free if you sleep on deck. We can catch up on news and have all the fish and seaweed cakes we can eat.'

Winston shook his head. 'That's very kind of you, but I'm afraid my master gets seasick, and he doesn't like fish.'

'It must be annoying, watching him eat like that while you get by on whatever's left,' said Porrel.

Resentment flared deep within Winston for a moment.

'Actually, why not?' he said. 'Thank you, Stanni. Offer accepted.'

Back at the tavern, Winston presented Faramond with the choice between one day on a ship and five days' walking. Faramond chose the ship, so Winston and his master were on the *Salt Dragon* when it sailed on the evening tide.

Within the first hour rough weather set in, and Winston watched without sympathy as the wizard dashed for the railing. He almost made it before throwing up the poached eggs with rich golden yolks, thick herbed bacon, crisp potato fritters, slices of soft crusty stone bread and golden gooseberry pie served with corn syrup, whipped cream and custard sauce, and the platter of light fluffy cakes.

'I suppose some fish will be grateful,' said Winston. Beside him on the quarterdeck, Stanni was doing a shift at the ship's wheel.

'You handle the rough weather well. You could be a sailor if you ever get tired of magic,' said Stanni.

'I'm fine with magic. It's the people who teach me magic that are the problem,' Winston said, gesturing down at Faramond by the light from the mainmast lantern. 'Why is there a rope tied to his leg?'

'Every so often there's a really large wave that comes out of nowhere. It washes over the decking and carries off anything that's not tied down.'

'Including passengers throwing up over the side?'

'Aye. We call them assassin waves.'

As if on cue, an enormous wave crashed over the middle deck of the ship. When the water drained away through the scuppers, Winston saw that Faramond was missing.

'Like that one?' asked Winston.

'Aye. Go below and tell the mate that we've got a floater.'

Five of the crew were needed to help Winston drag Faramond back onto the ship. The force of the assassin wave had literally ripped his robe right off his body. The wizard had been wearing nothing underneath, so he looked like some pale, monstrous frog as the cargo crane lifted him from the water by the rope attached to his leg. Stanni laughed so much that she collapsed to the deck, kicking her legs in the air. Winston speedily left the deck and took over the ship's wheel.

The short voyage to Haldan stretched into two days of rough weather, and Faramond didn't eat for the entire time. Stanni gave Winston some old clothes that the sailors used for cleaning rags, and by the time Haldan was in sight Winston had sewn together a very large sailor suit for his master to wear. All that Faramond had left to prove that he was not a sailor down on his luck was his red pointy hat. Winston had stowed this in the cargo hold with his pack and wayfarer's staff. The saddlebags and Faramond's staff were back in Loseros, and probably on sale in the market.

When the small ship docked, Faramond got down on his hands and knees and kissed the pier's decking, then spent two days eating in the city's taverns. He had spent the money that Winston had loaned him, and was holding out his hand for more when Winston decided to tell him that they were approaching a financial crisis.

'Master, we have just enough silver to hire a sand cart and buy food for the journey to the sanctum,' he said.

'What good is a sand cart if I'm starving to death?' demanded Faramond, snatching the purse from Winston.

'Do you have a way to cross a hundred miles

of desert on foot, with no food and nothing but water to drink?'

Faramond thought about this for a moment. They couldn't afford to be late for their meeting with the Guild Elders, and travelling on a sand cart was faster and far easier than walking. The wizard flung the purse back at Winston.

'Go find me a sand cart,' muttered Faramond, as if it had been his idea. 'And don't forget to buy proper food.'

Sand carts were a convenient way to travel when the land was too barren for horses or donkeys to forage. The cart was just that, a cart. For a fee, one employed a gutter wizard to cast imps into the hollow wheels, and these ran around inside, driving the cart forward. They usually took about a week to break free and escape, but that would be enough to reach the sanctum. All one had to do was steer. Faramond cast his own imps into the four wheels, causing him to lose weight to offset the magic, but a flying carpet would require a lot more weight to be sacrificed, and riding a swaying camel would be too much like being back on the fishing boat.

Faramond sat on the driver's board and steered the sand cart for the first hundred yards, but cries like 'Oi, there's a sailor wearing a wizard's hat and driving a cart!' prompted him to hand control over to Winston and hide inside the cart's canvas cabin. They were travelling without an armed escort, which was foolish, but they were on a cart that rolled along without any sort of animal pulling it, so ambushers instantly knew that at least one wizard was probably on board. Wizards never bothered to carry much in the way of gold, or even silver. Besides, the good ones could cast very cruel spells, such as relocating a thief's vocal cords at the other end of their digestive tract.

The Countercasts' Guild Sanctum was in a part of the desert between the Alberkin Mountains and the north-east coast of the continent. Winston and Faramond deliberately skirted the Barrenlands because the outlaws who lived there were so wild that they'd even attack a wizard if the day had been boring. It was a journey of a hundred miles, and Faramond was not enjoying it. The desert was very hot, Winston could only afford cheap food, and there was nothing to drink but two skins of rainwater.

There were no taverns where Faramond could get large, civilised meals, and anyway, there was hardly any money left. Faramond ate the five days of stores on the first day, and when he opened Winston's backpack, he discovered that the youth had packed only smoked fish and rainwater for the journey.

'You did that on purpose,' he shouted, striking Winston over the head with a smoked cod. 'You know I can't stand fish!'

'But Master, I like fish.'

Faramond snatched up the fish and flung them out of the wagon. Winston sighed but wasn't really concerned. Hidden under his robes were two more smoked cod, tied to the drawstring of his trousers. Over the next four days Faramond grew so hungry that he even tried to eat the straps of his apprentice's backpack. Winston only took his smoked cod out when he heard Faramond snoring in the back of the cart.

Chapter Three

They reached Olga's Oasis on the third day. Here a few palms and acaciallen trees survived the extremes of the desert, huddled around a small pool fed by an underground spring. Beside it was a perfectly round tower of black stone, capped by a dome.

Faramond was hesitant. 'I don't like it,' he said as they approached. 'That thing was not there when I last came this way.'

'When was that?' asked Winston.

'Five years ago.'

'It could've been built in five years.'

'It must be a hundred feet high, with a diameter of at least fifty. Who builds something like that in the middle of a desert?'

'We could just steer around it.'

'No! I've not eaten for four days, and there are dates on those palms. Stop at the oasis pool, but don't go anywhere near the tower.'

Winston steered them in amongst the palm trees and locked the brake lever. As Faramond climbed down from the cart, the wooden handhold broke under his weight. 'Argh!' he screamed as he toppled like a skittle.

Winston helped him up.

'You got fleeced on this one, boy,' Faramond growled, holding up the splintered handhold.

'But you approved it, Master.'

'Don't you argue with me!' he shouted, flinging the broken handhold at Winston.

While Winston filled the water skins from the pool, Faramond tried to climb one of the palm trees. He got about a foot off the ground before giving up and tracing a spell and casting a faint, glowing extension of his right arm. The palms turned out to be coconut palms, but Faramond was desperate for anything less chewy than leather straps. After the fifteenth coconut he settled down in the shade and closed his eyes.

With the water skins full and Faramond asleep, Winston turned his attention to the tower. He had watched stone buildings being rebuilt when he was younger; it happened a lot in Loseros with the sea advancing. There were always odd chips of stone, clumps of mortar and sometimes even broken tools left lying about when the work was done. There was nothing in the sand at the base of this tower. He walked around it, very slowly. There was nothing on the side facing away from the oasis. Faramond was still asleep when he completed his circuit of the tower, and everything was the same as before . . . except that there now was a door facing the oasis.

Am I being watched? Winston wondered as he approached the door. But the place had no windows, or even eye slits. He took a proper look at the nails in the timbers of the door. They were all in the shape of little golden eyes, with green jewels for pupils. So, someone really was watching, and that someone had just put a door in the wall.

Winston knocked. The door seemed solid enough, but the wood had a texture more like pottery than timber. He was about to knock again when arms burst through the wood before he even had a chance to gasp with fright. They were smooth arms as pale as moonlight, and they wrapped around Winston as tightly as iron chains. As he drew breath to scream, he had a feeling that thousands of ants were running races across his skin, under his clothes, and then he was drawn right through the wood of the door.

Coming to the conclusion that screaming himself hoarse wasn't helpful, Winston opened his eyes. He was kneeling on something soft, white, warm and pleasantly scented. His hands were over his head, but he was fairly sure that they'd be no protection against anything in there that wanted to eat him. He straightened himself and saw that he was kneeling on the palm of a hand the size of the town square in Loseros. The light was pale and weak, as if from a quarter moon, and seemed to be coming from nowhere in particular. He looked up. He would've described the face that looked down at him as beautiful, except the word that entered his mind and refused to go away was *enormous*.

'Welcome to my tower, Winston Spellwyn,' said a voice like thunder made of velvet.

Winston gulped.

'You are overawed, perhaps even intimidated. I can cure that.'

An instant later, Winston found himself

standing beside a woman his own height, no more than ten years older than him. He remained alarmed, however, because they were about a thousand feet up and standing on nothing at all. Again, Winston managed not to scream. For the sake of my sanity and to retain control of my bladder, I'm going to treat this as a dream, he decided. He noticed that the woman's gown seemed to be made of green quicksilver.

'Come with me, I have something important to show you,' she said.

They floated downwards, and Winston now saw that Olga's Oasis was below them, with Faramond still sleeping in the shade of a tree. They flew out over the desert, more swiftly than any bird could. Ahead of them, Winston saw a dark carpet that resembled the surface of a pond in a rainstorm. It was moving across the sand in the direction of the oasis.

'That is a chitterling swarm,' said the woman. 'Have you ever seen one?'

'I've read of them.'

'Someone saw a swarm and lived to write about it? That sounds unlikely.'

'Vardulas the Timid was in a caravan and

managed to empty a wooden chest and hide in it until the chitterling attack was over. When he emerged, the entire caravan was just skeletons of men and camels.'

'Ah, clever of him. Eventually, the chitterlings will go back to the Badlands, but right now, they're bad neighbours. Let us get rid of them before they eat your master.'

Winston saw that she was holding a phial about the size of his thumb. This she handed to him, and he held it up to his face. A tiny creature was held within by a cork. It was human in shape, except that it had folded, bat-like wings instead of arms, and talons similar to those of an eagle, for feet. There were claws like hands on the first joint of both wings, and it had a tail about half the length of its body. It was entirely covered in short red fur, except for the much longer red hair on its head. What Winston had taken for horns were actually pointed ears, and his general impression was that it was female. The fur made her look as if she was wearing very tight clothes. She glared up at him and snarled, baring a pair of impressive fangs.

'She's beautiful!' exclaimed Winston.

The creature blinked at him then stared back in astonishment. The woman beside him was astonished as well.

'That's the first time I have heard of an iffryt described as beautiful,' she said. 'Now watch, see what the little horror can do.'

The woman traced a spell in the air, then took the phial from him, handed him the cork and shook the little creature onto her palm. Winston recognised the spell as a symbol for *cat*. She closed her fist over it, then opened her hand to reveal dark red powder on her palm. This she poured onto the swarm of chitterlings. As it fell, the powder formed into a red cat. This in itself would have been remarkable, except that this cat was the size of the small ship on which his sister was a sailor. It devoured the chitterlings in a feeding frenzy.

'Imagine what it could do to a human,' said the woman.

'I'd rather not,' Winston stammered.

'Chitterlings were once the weapon of a kingdom so ancient that even its name has been lost. The king's wizards turned the swarm loose against the armies of his enemies, not realising that the more they ate, the stronger they became. They're like rats, but with jaws strong enough to bite through a thick iron nail. After feeding on the enemy army, they became too powerful to control.'

'You mean they turned on their creators?'

'They did just that. Fortunately for everyone else on the continent, they were conjured and formed to dwell in the kingdom of their masters and nowhere else. That is what we know of as the Badlands today. Occasionally they get hungry enough to venture out here, but they sicken and die unless they return to the Badlands after a few days.'

They watched as the iffryt-cat bolted down the last of the chitterlings, then the woman traced another spell in the air and held out the phial. The cat dissolved into red smoke that flowed up from the desert and into the phial.

'Cork,' said the woman. Winston handed it back to her.

She held the phial up to show him that the iffryt was again a tiny red creature confined inside. She closed her hand over the phial, and when she opened it again, both jar and iffryt were gone. Winston noticed that the desert was fading and being replaced by the interior of the tower. A spiral staircase wound against the inner wall, leading to a great circular gallery. At the top was a thin arch of stone steps, and below the arch was a disk of nothingness.

'This is the image of a place of great power, Winston,' said the woman. 'It is the Blackstone Tower in the Harst Mountains. That dark thing is a portal to another world, a world where only iffryts live. Power flows out of that world and into ours. The Summoner wizards use that power. It's why their castings and enchantments outclass Countercast magic so very much.'

They descended to within a few feet of the floor, and now Winston saw that it was covered with bones. Armour and weapons were scattered amid the bones, but every sword, battle axe, shield and lance had been broken, and both chainmail and plate armour had been ripped apart. Winston was astonished to see that two of the skeletons had come from medium-sized dragons, and several sets of bones were from creatures that weren't at all familiar to him.

'Heroes, wizards, maidens pure of heart,

dragons, trained hunting dogs, eagles, apes strong enough to rip your arms off, and creatures so small that they hoped not to be noticed: all tried to breach the tower, but none lived.'

'Does a demon live here?' asked Winston.

'The tower is an ifftyt, Winston. The Summoners used to be its masters, until a foolish apprentice learned the Spell of Yoal and stole the Imperium Key, long, long ago. Come with me, meet him.'

They drifted across to the base of the spiral staircase. A few steps up lay yet another skeleton. Judging by the remnants of cloth strewn about the skeleton, it had been a young male. His skull was crushed, and Winston saw that most of his ribs were broken as well. Amid the bones of one hand was a complex and ornate key made of black metal. A green jewel in the shape of an eye was mounted within the lattice of its teeth, and a chain of the same black metal was wrapped around the bones of his wrist.

'Whoever wears that key controls the portal,' said the woman.

She reached out for the key, but her fingers passed through it.

'None of this is real,' Winston said.

'Not so, or perhaps not entirely so. The chitterlings and the desert were real, but this is my mind's image of how it probably looks inside the Blackstone Tower. Ah, I see that Faramond is awake.'

'He's probably hungry.'

'Alas, that is the price of power in Countercast wizardry. For now, that is enough for you, Apprentice Winston. In a day or two we shall meet again, and there will be more.'

Whatever the source of light might have been, it was abruptly extinguished. Winston felt hands pushing against his back, then he was through the door and back in the bright sunlight of the desert.

Faramond watched Winston emerge through the timber of the door. 'You got in!' he exclaimed.

'Sort of,' replied Winston.

'You did or you didn't, idiot boy!' Faramond's eyes grew wide. 'Not using one of your infernal illegal spells, I hope?'

Winston indicated the door. 'Of course not. I just knocked.'

Faramond's eyes now squinted. 'There was no door when I inspected the place.'

'It just . . . appeared.'

'I can see it now!' fumed Faramond. 'What was inside?'

'There was a woman—'

'A woman?' Faramond repeated, eyebrows furrowing.

'A rather beautiful woman,' Winston elaborated needlessly.

'She might have been a demon. Young men who consort with demons get torn to pieces and eaten.'

'She said there's a swarm of chitterlings nearby.'

'Chitterlings? They're extinct. She saw you coming, boy.'

Faramond settled himself beside the tree again, but Winston went over to the cart.

'I say we camp here for the night. It's too hard to sleep with the cart rumbling along.'

'But you have eaten all the coconuts, and there's food at the sanctum.'

'Food!' exclaimed Faramond, struggling to his feet. 'If you drive the cart all night we can be at the sanctum in time for lunch tomorrow. What are you waiting for, wretched boy? Get on the cart!'

Five years and six months more of this, Winston thought. After that, he would be a fully qualified journeyman wizard and could hire his services out to whoever could pay. But why bother, when he could get a job as a cabin boy aboard Stanni's ship whenever he wanted? He supposed it was because magic could be so much fun.

Winston climbed onto the cart and released the brake. The cart rumbled into motion.

'Stop! Stop! Fool!' shouted Faramond, who had not yet boarded the cart.

Almost as much fun as antagonising Faramond, thought Winston as he engaged the brake.

The Prince-Adept, Thomarn of Yorta, had been an apprentice barely two years when he challenged the Blackstone Tower and hence made a name for himself, thought Winston. He barely heard Faramond, back in the covered tray, shouting that he was the stupidest apprentice in the history of magic. Of course, Thomarn was never seen again but that's not the point. Doing something interesting is far more important than merely living.

'Oi, Winston,' Faramond called.

'Aye, Master?'

'The tower,' said Faramond fearfully. 'It's vanished.'

They arrived at the sanctum mid-afternoon the following day. The walls were of black marble, cut to look ugly and threatening, and turrets jutted skyward like the clawed fingers of a djinn the size of a mountain. The building seemed to drink light from the very air itself. A wide moat of turgid green water surrounded it.

It was said that were it not for the wizards who lived there, the Barrenlands would spread across the entire world. It was also said, by other wizards, that those of the Countercasts' Guild Sanctum spread the rumour so that people would pay them to do whatever they did to control the Barrenlands and hold them back.

'It's the stuff of myths, of course,' Faramond scoffed. 'But never say that in front of the peasants or they'll get ideas.'

As they approached the parking embankment, Winston hauled on the brake lever, decreasing their speed. When the sand cart came to rest against the buffers, he checked the imps in the wheels.

'They're just about spent,' he said. 'They'll be gone by the time we get out – *if* we get out.'

'I cast them to last seven days,' retorted Faramond.

'Then why have they lasted only five?'

'Because you drove them too hard, stupid boy.' He cast a black look at Winston. 'That, or they're part of your "union" movement.'

Winston would not be baited in an exchange he knew he would lose. Instead, he looked up with foreboding at the impossibly large building. He knew that it was within those walls that his fate would be decreed, yet the woman from the tower said that they would meet again. Would it be here? She seemed to be friendly. Was it the sort of friendly that a fox is with a chicken? he wondered.

Faramond climbed from the sand cart's tray very carefully, then stood looking up at the tower with his hands on his hips. Out of nowhere, a strong wind suddenly pushed at him from behind, as if reminding him of why they were there. The wizard cast a suspicious look at his apprentice.

'I didn't do it,' said Winston, shrugging.

'Come along,' Faramond growled, glancing about. 'Remember, the Lost Spell of Yoal was devised by an ancestor of the Sorceress Yolantha, the leader of our elders. The spell was lost by an apprentice like you, so she doesn't like apprentices.'

'Wasn't that apprentice from the Guild of Summoners?'

'She used to be a Summoner.'

'But you said the spell doesn't exist,' he said.

'I'm telling you the story; I didn't say it was *true*!' snapped Faramond. He ushered his apprentice forward. 'Hurry along.'

They reached the edge of the moat. The drawbridge was down, but an enormous serpentine neck wound around it, and a head about the size of their sand cart looked down at them. Unlike the dragon Griffid, this thing had no horns, ears, crests or decoratively-flared nostrils. It was a snake magnified about a thousand times over.

Not really real, thought Winston, realising that he could see the sanctum's walls through the dripping reptile.

'I yield to the slightest touch, I am never seen, yet I eat mountains,' it declared in a voice like a barrel being rolled from a cart to a tavern.

A riddle? thought Winston. That one's easy.

'No, no, you're supposed to ask me the one about the hole in your purse,' Faramond snapped.

'My spell has been reconfigured,' hissed the serpent.

'It has? What idiot authorised that?'

'Lady Yolantha.'

Silence. Then, 'Oh. Well, why wasn't I told?'

'You are being told now. What is the answer?' demanded the serpent.

Faramond tapped at his bald head, as if urging his brain to wake up and help him.

'Ah, the tread of travellers' boots over the ages?' he ventured.

'You can see boots treading, and the tread of a boot is hard, not soft and yielding. Besides, travellers don't walk on mountain peaks.'

'Well, maybe not, but you must admit that—'

The enormous jaws gaped wide, the head

lunged forward and Faramond was snatched off the bank. Winston could hear muffled shrieking as a large lump travelled down the serpent's neck, wound around the drawbridge and disappeared into the green water beneath.

That was a rather final conclusion, Winston thought, taking a pointless step back.

The serpent turned its gaze on him.

'I neither move nor fight, yet I can bring down the walls of the mightiest castle more surely than a siege engine,' the creature's voice boomed.

'The roots of a tree,' said Winston, who had seen a great number of buildings destroyed by trees growing in Kalderial.

'Very good, you may pass.'

'Wait!' called Winston. 'What about my master?'

'He failed the test.'

'And if I answer his riddle?'

'Your master is worthless. Aren't you better rid of him?'

'I swore loyalty to him until my indenture is served out,' Winston reasoned.

The serpent's eyes narrowed. 'You shall follow your master if you fail.'

Winston took a deep breath, thinking that it might well be his last. 'The wind wears down mountains, yet cannot be seen and has the softest of touches.'

Surprised at this correct response, the serpent hissed and then turned to vapour. There was a loud bang as the air rushed in to fill the space where it had been, and bubbles erupted within the moat. Amid the turbulent and spitting greenish water bobbed Faramond. Winston hurried onto the drawbridge, extended his wayfarer's staff down to the wizard, then dragged him to the bank of the moat.

'Stupid, stupid boy, releasing me into that vile water!' shouted Faramond. 'The sanctum's privies all empty into the moat. The thing is one huge sewer.'

'My apologies, Master, but—'

'Oh. just shut up and get out of my way!' Faramond spluttered.

Dripping greenish water, slime and waterweeds, Faramond strode across the drawbridge amid a cloud of flies. At the base of the sanctum wall, he traced a symbol on the stone. The symbol glowed for a moment, then the featureless stone became a door. Faramond pushed at it, and it swung back easily.

'The Guild hearings are always pompous events, but these people have a lot of power,' the wizard whispered as they walked in. 'Be polite, because they can ruin us, even destroy us.'

Faramond angrily batted at the flies as he walked, but he walked slowly, even reluctantly. This was an organisation that didn't accept defiance. Nobody but a sanctioned guild member could perform magic unless they had a licence from the Guild Elders. Their price was high, but it guaranteed an easy life. Winston had done his magical experiments under the sponsorship of Faramond, but they had been unsanctioned. That meant both would probably share the blame and the punishments.

The stone doorway boomed shut behind them. Far ahead, the flame of a solitary torch danced, lighting their way along dry, cold flagstones. Faramond ushered Winston ahead of him, and at the end of the corridor a massive oak door below the torch swung open without needing a spell traced or a word of power spoken.

'Do come in,' said the voice of an unseen watcher.

Faramond fought the urge to say something annoying. Everything about the Guild Elders irked him, mostly their power and their contempt for fellow wizards. Wizard and apprentice entered, and Winston saw that a reception delegation was already gathered to greet them. They were seated on a semicircle of chairs.

'Apprentice Winston, these are Ocularen of Cirrum, Chief Inquisitor, and Yolantha of Yoal, the High Sorceress, and the seven senior elders,' said Faramond. 'Show them the respect that you never show me, for they can see into your soul.'

Winston hid his surprise. Indeed, he already knew the woman.

Yolantha raised an eyebrow and a faint smile lifted the corners of her blood-red lips. The robe she wore now was green velvet embroidered in gold, with sigils older than any empire on the surface of the world. A brocade cowl that would have cost more than Winston's meals for a year cast half her face in a disturbing shadow.

Faramond wrung his hands, overcome either

by her beauty or with terror.

'I see you have invited some friends,' said Yolantha. 'Sorry, but only Winston is allowed in here.'

She snapped her fingers, and a swarm of small bats descended from the rafters above, whirled around Faramond – snapping the flies out of the air – then flew back up to their roosts.

'Why are you wearing a sailor suit, Faramond?' Yolantha now asked.

'This miserable boy will be the death of me,' the wizard grumbled for the benefit of those gathered there. 'He got us aboard a ship with a storm on the way. I was washed overboard, so I had to struggle out of my robes and abandon them so I could swim. Fortunately, I am a strong swimmer and I climbed back aboard wearing only my hat.'

'My imagination does not dare conjure that image,' the sorceress replied. 'You will be given a new robe before you leave, I'll not have Guild members looking like the comedy act of some travelling carnival.'

'Ladyship, I'm deeply honoured.'

'And you will pay for it.'

'Of course, of course.' He bowed hurriedly.

Winston was genuinely impressed by the illustrious company. While he and Faramond only wore clean robes when Winston could no longer stand the smell from the laundry basket and washed them, these wizards might have just stepped out of a tailor's shop. Those seated to either side of the High Sorceress wore black robes of silk that swallowed light, and these were gathered about their substantial waists by sashes as red as arterial blood. Unlike those attending her, Yolantha was as lean as a panther that preferred to hunt only the fastest gazelles. None of them looked any older than Faramond, which confirmed Winston's theories about the health hazards of being a Countercast wizard.

Although he and Faramond lived in a palace, Winston had improvised the furniture, the original furniture having been looted long ago. The furnishings here were the sort that only the genuinely rich and powerful could afford. Tapestries by master weavers and embroiderers filled the spaces on the walls between alarmingly lifelike carvings of creatures that he had not even known existed. Each sculpted head was crowned with a torch where cold, green flames danced and swayed. All the chairs were high-backed, carved from ebony, inlaid with gold and emeralds, and upholstered with a cloth that seemed more like shadow than fabric.

Winston was wondering if the chairs were also comfortable to sit on when he realised he was being spoken to.

'We are met this day to consider a matter of life and death,' said the High Sorceress, staring at her guests.

The wizards attending her nodded, but one man was snoring softly. Yolantha raised a hand and snapped her fingers. The chair swallowed the sleeper.

'Beds are for sleeping, chairs are for sitting up and paying attention,' she continued. 'My chairs don't like people using them to doze.' Her voice was as serious as a list of death penalties.

The remaining wizards were now sitting up very straight, and with their eyes wide open from terror. No one expressed the slightest surprise, knowing that Yolantha was pricklier than a mace studded with nails.

'You are the apprentice of Faramond?' the

High Sorceress asked.

'Speak up, boy!' Faramond said before Winston could react.

Winston nodded, not daring to speak.

'You seem to have some very clever ideas.'

Winston risked a smile.

'Nothing annoys me more than a wizard with ideas.'

Winston ceased smiling.

'How would you like to perform a task for me?'

'Great and most awesome lady, this miserable boy is—' was as far as Faramond got.

'Faramond, my chairs are always hungry.'

'Apologies,' whispered Faramond, bowing again as deeply as he was able.

'Winston, what do you know of the Blackstone Tower?' asked Yolantha.

'It's a tower deep in the Harst Mountains. That, and that it's black.'

'What did I just say about my chairs always being hungry?'

'Apologies,' whispered Winston with a very low bow, recalling that it had worked for Faramond. 'It's a very potent magical site, and nobody has ever breached it.'

'You have done a lot of clever but unauthorised studies,' said Yolantha.

With that she glided to her feet like a cat that had just noticed breakfast emerging from a mouse hole.

'Come along,' she said. 'Oh, and Faramond Erris?'

'Yes, Ladyship?'

'Take a bath.'

The flagstone on which Faramond had been standing swung out from under him, and the wizard vanished into the chamber below with an echoing scream. The following splash was so great that some of the water reached the floor of the audience chamber.

Winston was led into a smaller chamber, which contained a single bench upholstered in the same deadly black fabric as the chairs. Yolantha sat down and gestured to the other end. Winston joined her, but very hesitantly. Although the air was cold, he was perspiring.

'Winston, what can you tell me about the wizards beyond that door?'

'They are rather . . . large, and not in the best of health.'

'And not pleasing to look upon. You, on the other hand, are very young and probably have more talent than all of them put together. You have a lean, hungry look, and I like all things lean and hungry.'

Yolantha reached into the fabric of the bench as if it were black quicksilver and pulled out a pendant on a chain.

'Now tell me, what is this?' she asked.

'A wizard's pendant.'

'The pendant of a graduate wizard, Winston.' She tossed him the pendant. 'Consider that as payment in advance of services to be rendered. Tell me, what might I want in exchange?'

Winston thought through some possibilities.

'Some great feat of bravery and enchantment?' he offered. It seemed a safe sort of reply.

'Close enough. I have read the paper you presented at the Young Magical Apprentices conference. You have rediscovered the art of making use of another wizard's magical . . .'

'Body fat?' ventured Winston.

'Such a crass term, I must think of a more

elegant one. When casting spells with our techniques, fat gets burned away first, then muscle, then organs that can be spared, then those organs that are rather more important.'

'Like the heart?'

'Yes, and you wouldn't last long without one. The Lost Spell of Yoal allowed wizards to share their resources, as you discovered. It can also do much, much more. I am descended from the legendary wizard Yoal, and I have managed to reconstruct parts of the spell, just as you have.'

'So . . . you don't mind me doing what I did?'

'Between you and me alone, no. Progress is all about breaking rules. I break rules all the time, but enough of that. Just now we have a . . . delicate situation. The Summoner wizards have actually appealed to us humble Countercast wizards for help. Can you believe it?'

'No,' Winston answered. It seemed to him to be what Yolantha probably wanted to hear.

'What do you know about Summoners?'

'They are wizards who enslave iffryts as a source of power?'

'The very same. They expelled me from their Guild. Did you know that?'

'Foolish of them,' Winston ventured.

'Their elders said I was learning too much, too fast, and that I was not developing enough wisdom to keep pace with my powers. I smuggled out a single iffryt when I left.'

'The girl in the phial?'

Yolantha held up the phial. 'The very same. She is the source of most of my powers, although I can draw on my own Countercast wizards if the need is pressing.'

She held up her other hand and snapped her fingers. Immediately the room became what looked like a library, except that instead of books, the shelves were lined with little corked phials. Only one in ten contained an iffryt – the others held red dust. A tall, gaunt man stood before Winston and Yolantha. He was dressed in black silks, but that was all Winston noticed about his clothing. It was so black that he seemed to be wearing shadows.

Winston stood up at once and bowed.

'Archasin Dral, this is Winston of Shop Spellwyn, most recent provisional graduate of our guild,' Yolantha said without getting up.

'Make this brief,' said Archasin. 'Maintaining

this image is immensely draining.'

'Archasin is over two hundred miles away, in the city of Varlin,' Yolantha explained.

'I am prepared to let you have one iffryt for your scheme,' Archasin continued, gesturing to the shelves behind him. 'Just point to your choice, and I shall send it to you by the fastest merchant ship currently docked in the harbour.'

Winston looked over the iffryts, which snarled and bared their teeth at him from within their little phials. He looked back to the phial Yolantha held. The iffryt inside was staring at him, but otherwise crouched perfectly still.

'What about that one?' he asked.

'Elvar?' exclaimed Yolantha. 'Why her?'

'She's already here. I can begin work on your task at once, instead of waiting for the ship to reach Haldan,' said Winston, hoping that a display of eagerness would please Yolantha. 'The winds are not favourable at this time of year. It'd take at least three weeks to arrive.'

'Keen boy,' said Archasin.

'I will want one of your iffryts to replace her,' said Yolantha.

'Why? You stole Elvar in the first place.'

'And now I am your only hope!' snapped Yolantha. 'The Summoners are in decline, Winston. Their iffryts are crumbling, not one of them is less than three thousand years old. They lost the Imperium Key, and thus control of the Blackstone Tower.'

'I pledge one of my remaining iffryts if your Elvar is lost,' said Archasin.

'Can I ask what the Imperium Key does?' asked Winston.

'It controls the Blackstone Tower's portal,' said Archasin. 'For three thousand years it has been trapped inside the tower in the hands of a dead boy. Without it, I cannot summon new iffryts from the world on the other side of the portal.'

'But don't the energies from that world still flow through?'

'Yes.'

'Yes, but for one important detail,' said Yolantha. 'When the last of their iffryts crumble, the portal will collapse and the energies will cease flowing. I'm doing you a great favour, Archasin, and I expect to be taken back into your order and made your successor when Winston emerges from the tower with the Imperium Key.'

'I have already agreed to that,' muttered Archasin.

'Very well, I shall concede,' said Yolantha. 'Winston, you may take Elvar and leave today.'

Without another word, Archasin raised a hand and snapped his fingers. The room once again became Yolantha's audience chamber. Yolantha traced the spell for *chain* in the air and closed her fingers around Elvar's phial. When she opened her fist again there was a gold chain attached to it. She stood, languidly yet threateningly, like a snake uncoiling, then draped the phial around Winston's neck.

'My powers will be greatly diminished without Elvar at my command,' she said. 'Do not set her free. Only I know the castings to control her.'

'But if she does escape?' asked Winston.

'She will start by tearing you to pieces.'

'Oh.'

'Then she will probably flee to the island of Dracondas, where dragons rule. There is a small group of escaped iffryts cowering there. They are worth a fortune to any Summoner who can sneak past the dragons and trap them.'

'Ladyship, may I ask why you took control of this guild of . . .'

Winston struggled to find a polite word.

'Gluttons?' asked Yolantha, then laughed. 'Because it was easy, and because some power is better than no power. Help me gain control of the Summoners, Winston.'

'But Lord Archasin already said he would make you his successor.'

'Combine the Imperium Key with the reliable powers of Countercast magic and I cannot be stopped by any Summoner. They don't suspect as much, because Countercasts are such a joke, yet the lost spell will make all the difference. Complete the lost spell, secure me that key, and I shall be very grateful, Winston. Your wildest dreams cannot show you how pleasant life could be as my ally. Come along now, let us present you to the elders.'

Yolantha had an arm around Winston's shoulders as they walked out of the audience chamber. Faramond was back, now dressed in a new wizard's robe of red and gold. Water still dripped from his beard. He goggled at Winston and Yolantha, then scowled.

'I wish to present Provisional Wizard Winston,' Yolantha declared to the elders. 'He is now a graduate and provisional member of our guild, but will be made a full member upon completing the task I am about to set him.'

Faramond looked shocked, while the others merely nodded. Some smiled. A few smirked. Yolantha sauntered over to the vacant chair and took a staff from behind it.

'Catch!' she called, tossing it to Winston. 'Every wizard should have one of these.'

Winston knew that Faramond's staff was back in Loseros. The wizard had borrowed Winston's wayfarer's staff, hoping that the sorceress wouldn't notice.

'You are about to be sent on a great and dangerous task, Winston,' Yolantha continued. 'If you succeed, we can't have people saying a mere apprentice managed to do what we wizards couldn't, can we?'

'But what about the remaining years of my apprenticeship?'

'You will spend them serving me.'

For some reason, working in squalor for Faramond seemed a lot less frightening, but Winston had the sense not to say so.

Yolantha turned her attention to Faramond, asking him to give an account of what he had been doing in the five years since he had last visited the sanctum. Most of what he said was fabricated, and Winston suspected Yolantha already knew as much. His eyes strayed to a portrait high above the gallery. It was of Lord Cabal, once the supreme lord of all the magical guilds, but now long dead.

Lord Cabal gazed from the picture, displaying a cadaverous and blanched face heavy with an ancient power. A white wisp of a goatee flowed from his chin and long silver hair hung limp across his shoulders. Hanging about his neck was the Imperium Key.

Winston was struck by a sense of familiarity. He somehow knew this man, although he was long dead.

'Winston!'

Faramond's voice brought Winston back from his reverie. 'The chalice, boy. Tell them about it.'

'Chalice?' asked Winston.

'The jug then, if you want to call it that. You paid the dragon's fee with it.'

'Tell me about it,' said Yolantha, turning to Winston with a wide smile.

'I think it was an old rhyming jug, but the quatrain on it was incomplete. There were only two lines.'

'Its companion, Provisional Wizard Winston – where is it? Faramond said it is lost.'

'I believe so, Ladyship.'

'One jug lost, the other in a dragon's hoard,' mused Yolantha. 'That could make me angry, but the inscription could please me greatly.'

'Why is lost, but shall be found, see to my skip above the ground,' recited Winston.

Yolantha took a step backwards, her mouth open and her eyes wide.

'Is that it?' she gasped. 'Are you sure?'

'I learned enough of the old language to translate it.'

Yolantha put a hand to her forehead and rubbed as if she had a headache in the making.

'Faramond, any wizard should have been able to recognise the importance of that jug. Get it back from the dragon and find the other or I'll make *you* Winston's apprentice.'

And here I was thinking I was having a bad day, thought Winston.

'Anything else, m'lady?' Faramond fawned.

'Oh yes, that was the easy part. You must use the lost spell to get into Blackstone Mountain's tower. There you will find the skeleton of a boy, and amid his bones will be a key. Bring it to me.'

'As good as done,' babbled Faramond.

'To do as I have commanded, I shall give you both an incentive. Whoever presents me with the Imperium Key will get that vacant chair and become one of my Guild Elders. However, I also think you will need a little encouragement to try harder, and even to stay together and work as a team. Winston, when you leave these walls, you will be carrying a deadline curse. In two months, it will be set free.'

'Will it kill me?' the apprentice gasped.

'No, but it will make you seem delicious to everything dangerous and magical.'

Yolantha drew a glowing spell, kissed her fingertips and clapped. The scent of baking bread and roasting meat arose in Winston's nostrils.

'Notice that you smell delicious to yourself.

Exceed my deadline, and all things dreaded and dangerous will be able to smell you as well. Faramond, yours will be a shackle curse to your talented but undisciplined young apprentice.'

'What will it do?' the wizard babbled.

'Venture more than a few hundred paces from Winston – and find out.'

Yolantha traced a second spell, which slowly drifted down to the floor. She stamped it with her foot. Faramond yelped, then hopped about for a moment, as if he were barefoot on hot stones.

'That is all. You may go.'

Very slowly, and bowing at every step, Winston and Faramond backed away.

'You wretched boy,' Faramond muttered as they reached the doors. 'Got off lightly, we did. She fed that dotard wizard to his own chair, and he was more important than either of us.'

Faramond squeezed his eyes shut for a moment and tried to think calmly. 'I wonder what she's planning. It's unusual for her to be lenient. She let us walk out unscathed.'

'She seemed angrier at you, Master,' said Winston.

'Well, she cursed us both, so don't get cocky!'

All the while Winston's head was whirling with confusion. Yolantha had seemed so very familiar and confiding with him in the audience chamber, yet she had suddenly turned on him and cast the deadline curse. Why? She was offering him a lot, but perhaps the Guild of Summoners could offer more.

'Furthermore,' Faramond said, nudging Winston, 'she'll suspect that you'll keep the Imperium Key for yourself. She's cursed us to ensure you deliver it to her.'

'Or I could sell it to the highest bidder – the Summoners – and be protected from her,' Winston surmised.

Faramond winced. 'Wash your mouth out with soap, Winston Spellwyn.' He looked around fearfully and whispered, 'The walls have ears, you idiot!'

Chapter Four

Dusk had come and gone by the time Winston and Faramond emerged from the sanctum and returned to their sand cart. It now contained food, skins of rainwater and two purses of silver.

'Get it moving,' snapped Faramond.

'The imps have dissolved back into spirits.'

'The imps have dissolved, MASTER!' roared Faramond. 'You may be a provisional wizard, but as long as you're only provisional you're still my apprentice.'

'But you still need to cast more imps, *Master*.'

'Well, you're so clever, you find some way to get it moving!' shouted Faramond.

'Any way that I can? I know better ways to make a sand cart move.'

'Then use them.'

'You may not like—'

'I'll like whatever gets us away from here faster than our own feet.'

Winston held out his right hand, traced a spell above it with his left, then spoke words that were unfamiliar to Faramond. A ruby-red glow spread over his right hand.

'What have you done to your hand?' demanded the wizard. 'What were those words?'

'They were in an ancient book of medical castings that I found in the Kalderial palace. You were using the pages for toilet paper until I stole it.'

'Well, what of it? I'm no healer.'

Without a word of warning, Winston reached out and pressed his hand against Faramond's belly. Faramond shrieked with terror as the youth's hand passed through his robes. When Winston withdrew his hand, it was clenched into a fist, but there was no blood or scorching on either Winston or Faramond.

'By all the demons in everyone's hells, what did you just do?' screeched the wizard.

'I just took a little power for the sand cart.'

'My robes! They're looser!'

'Aye, Master, I changed some of your belly fat into an imp called an Aviornes. It will make the cart move.'

Faramond swooned. 'Wretched boy! But enough of that! Get us away from here before Lady Yolantha thinks of more confounded questions.'

Winston opened his right hand and pressed it against the side of the sand cart. The wheels promptly dissolved, and it crashed to the ground.

'What do you think you're *doing*?' demanded Faramond. 'We won't get far without wheels.'

'Of course we will, Master,' said Winston. 'Climb aboard.'

'Yolantha will regret making a wizard of you,' muttered Faramond, but he obediently heaved himself into the cart. Winston climbed into the driver's seat.

'Chicken up!' he called, and a pair of enormous chicken legs materialised beneath the cart, lifting it into the air.

'What in everyone's hells are you doing?' demanded Faramond. 'This thing wobbles worse than a camel.'

'Chicken walk!' commanded Winston. The enormous legs lumbered into motion, carrying the cart on top.

'This is worse than being at sea!' wailed Faramond. 'I'm going to be sick!' He made several gagging sounds and Winston prudently leaned away.

'Best do it over the side, Master.'

'Why give the thing legs?'

'So we don't have to stay on the roads. Wheels don't work terribly well on broken ground and sand dunes.'

Faramond had indeed been sick over the back of the cart several times by the time Winston stopped for the night. For the first time since leaving the ship, Faramond showed no interest in dinner. He was no longer throwing up when they set off the next morning, however, and seemed to be conquering his motion sickness.

'Your stomach seems happier about travelling on chicken legs, Master,' chirped Winston.

'That's because it's empty,' muttered Faramond.

'Be of good cheer, Master. On chicken legs we travel twice as fast, and in a straight line. You might even be eating in one of Haldan's taverns tonight.'

'I've been thinking about that inscription on the jug,' said Faramond, his voice still hoarse from heaving. 'It's word association. "Why" in the first line stands for the letter "Y" as in Yoal. That could mean that Yoal is lost but shall be found.'

'What about "See to my skip above the ground?"' asked Winston.

'Perhaps "See" stood for "C"?'

'C to my skip above the ground? Doesn't make sense.'

'Oh . . . well, let's discuss it later. More important things to worry about just now.'

'Like what, Master?'

'Like the squad of sand carts chasing us.'

'No problem, we don't have to travel on roads,' said Winston without turning.

'Neither do they. They're also on giant chicken legs.'

Only now did Winston turn, and he didn't like what he saw. 'Chicken jog!' shouted Winston to the legs.

'Desert cut-throats,' groaned Faramond.

'What are they doing with such advanced magic?' asked Winston. 'Aren't they just brigands?'

'Maybe, but they can hire wizards. Gutter wizards and journeyman wizards work for as little as three shillings a day.'

'Aren't there rules against that sort of thing?' asked Winston.

'Since when have you worried about rules?'

'When other people break them, Master. How are the odds?'

'Five carts, each with a driver and three rogues.'

'Chicken run!' called Winston.

The giant legs broke into a run, and for the first few minutes they held their distance from their pursuers.

'I know that you're meant to be a boy-wonder provisional wizard, but could a burned-out old failure wizard like me point out something important?' asked Faramond.

'What?' asked Winston.

'We're being herded into a blind gully.'

By now it was too late to do anything other than stop. Their pursuers surrounded them.

'You and your chicken legs,' muttered Faramond.

'Can I help it if they know the land and I don't, Master?'

The driver of the lead cart was a woman, which was a bad sign. Winston had heard that female brigands were more ferocious than the men. All of these brigands wore tunics of sun-bleached leather strapped by wide buckled belts. From these hung weather-beaten scabbards, but the swords were out and being pointed in the general direction of Winston and Faramond.

'Worthless merchants by the look of 'em,' called the tall, gaunt man commanding one of the other carts.

The woman moved her cart to flank them. She was dressed in much the same way as the other brigands, and there was something odd about the way her cart's chicken legs walked. They were thinner, wiry, almost athletic. Winston couldn't tell if her grin was friendly or was the sort that sharks have just before they bite. She was holding a sword, and strapped across her back was a short bow and a quiver of arrows. A bandana kept her long black hair clear of her eyes. Her teeth had been filed into points, possibly because she liked her meat raw, and preferably still alive.

'Wizards,' she said. 'Probably not carrying anything of value, but my cart wizard needs replacing.'

Winston figured she was referring to the wizard who looked like he was starving. They'd been using his magic too heavily and not feeding him enough. That meant he'd be at the end of his useful life, and probably his life in general.

The brigand carts edged closer and closer.

'Master, I need to draw on your resources again,' Winston whispered to Faramond.

'Like you did to create your infernal chicken legs? Absolutely not.'

'But we'll be forced into slave labour,' said Winston.

'All right, all right, just don't drain me to starvation.'

Winston wove his spell so fast he almost got the shape wrong. His hand glowed red, and he placed it against Faramond's belly. Once more, it shrank. Winston spread his fingers wide against the bottom of the cart.

'Chicken hawk!' he commanded. 'Attack.'

All at once the chicken legs beneath the cart became chicken hawk legs. The legs had talons a yard long, and were aware that five pairs of prey legs were encircling them. The chicken hawk casting had no eyes, but Winston had made himself part of his own cart, so that his eyes directed what followed.

The cart sprang upon the brigand woman's cart, slashing the chicken legs and tearing the cart's timbers to pieces. Any brigands who were in the way became pieces of brigands. The captive wizard leapt over the edge, landed on his feet in the sand and started running. The enraged brigand woman aimed an arrow at him, then changed her mind and shot at the sideboard of Winston's cart instead.

An enormous chicken hawk leg slashed at the next brigand cart within reach, and the blow annihilated it. Winston's chicken hawk cart then leapt onto the third cart and ripped it to pieces. It was all over within ten seconds. This had, however, been enough time for those driving the fourth and fifth carts to realise that they were well and truly outclassed. They turned their carts in opposite directions, commanding them to flee. Winston urged his chicken hawk cart to get moving as well.

After a few minutes they caught up with the fleeing slave wizard from the lead cart.

'Get away, I'd rather die than get into one of those things again!' he screamed.

Winston smiled at him. 'I just wondered if you would like a lift anywhere.'

An hour later Winston, Faramond and the slave wizard were in the desert brigands' stronghold. The guards who'd been left to defend the place had taken one look at the sand cart on eight-foot-high chicken hawk legs and locked themselves in the wine cellar.

'Theft is against the rules of our order,' said Faramond as the slave wizard loaded half a dozen bags of silver coins and a small bag of gold onto their cart.

'It's stolen,' said the slave wizard, whose name was Stylan. 'Can't steal stolen goods.'

'Yes you can!' scoffed Faramond, who had unpacked their basket of supplies and was munching his way through the contents.

'Who are we stealing it from then?' asked Stylan.

'Well, the brigands,' responded Faramond.

'But they stole it from the rightful owners.'

'Then we're stealing it from those people.'

'The brigands killed them.'

'Their heirs, then,' said Faramond, but with less certainty.

'Know their names?'

Winston had been listening to the exchange from the sand cart, where he had been removing arrows from the chicken hawk legs.

'You could visit some very expensive eateries when we reach Haldan,' he called.

Faramond didn't need to think about this for very long.

'You might have a point,' he said.

'I can recommend a very good place on the eastern edge of the market,' said Stylan. 'Their steak is marinated in vintage wine before going into the pies.'

'Vintage wine, you say?' asked Faramond, on the verge of drooling.

'Meantime, I'll stock up for the trip home,'

called Winston, removing the last arrow.

'In that case, I suppose we can consider the coins to be a long-lost treasure trove, and the property of whoever chances to find it,' Faramond conceded. 'You know, Winston, I've been thinking about the task ahead of us. Yolantha said the rhyme on the jar was incomplete.'

'Of course. It was said to be a quatrain. Quatrains have four lines, and two lines are missing.'

'What if Griffid has the missing lines somewhere?'

'Griffid? As in the dragon?'

'I don't know of any humans named Griffid. Don't worry about a thing, lad. Take me to him and I'll soon trick him into telling us.'

'But Master, Griffid is a dragon! Very large, breathes fire, flies, has legs with claws that make this cart's claws look like cloak pins.'

'Ah, but is his brain in a class equal to mine?'

Winston thought about that for a moment. 'No,' seemed the safest answer.

'There, what did I say?'

They climbed back into the cart. Winston commanded it to walk and Faramond settled down for the long and uncomfortable trip home.

'You two are going to challenge a dragon?' asked Stylan.

'Yes,' said Faramond.

'I just might take my share and set up a nice little bakery in Haldan,' Stylan decided. 'I was once a cook for a regional Countercasts' Sanctum.'

Being on the giant chicken hawk legs meant that they could travel in a straight line, so Winston steered the cart due south. After only three days they reached the village of Earthshift on the Harst River.

'Idiot boy!' roared Faramond. 'We were supposed to go to Haldan and set Stylan down there.'

'But Master, he can get passage on a barge to Haldan from here.'

'What do you use for brains, boy?' shouted Faramond, cuffing Winston across the ear. 'In these villages the taverns only serve pies made from whatever's left after all the good meat has been sliced off. Ears, eyes, gristle, guts and tails.'

'Kalderial is less than a day away, Master. I can catch a boar and roast it for tonight's dinner.'

The words *roast* and *boar* appealed to Faramond almost as much as the pies available in Haldan, and the ruins were closer than the port city. Leaving Winston to get the cart across the river and Stylan to find a barge going to Haldan, Faramond set off for the only tavern in Earthshift.

Earthshift's ferryman had a few doubts about transporting a cart supported by an enormous pair of bird legs and armed with talons longer than most swords, but Winston's stolen money eventually got the better of his fears. Getting Faramond away from his meal at the Bargeman's Delight was a lot harder.

'You just go ahead, boy,' said Faramond, between washing down the last of his beef and mushroom pie with a tankard of black ale and ordering a fourth pie. 'I'll follow in my own time.'

'But—'

'Don't argue with me, you donkey! Get your damn chicken cart over the water and await me on the southern bank. I've not had a proper meal in eleven days.'

'Aye, Master.'

Winston was on the ferry, halfway across the river, when a scream came echoing across the water.

'Be that the dragon Griffid in search of folk to eat?' asked the ferryman fearfully.

'No, that's just my master being reminded that he's been cursed,' sighed Winston.

'Then what's to be done, young sir?'

'First, deliver my chicken cart to the other side of the river, then take me back.'

The first thing that Winston saw as he entered the Bargeman's Delight was Faramond tied by both ankles and suspended upside down from a roof beam. There were charred footprints on the floorboards. On the floor beside the table where Faramond had been eating were his trail boots. Their soles had been burned away, as if he'd been standing on hot coals. His face was blood red.

'Winston, you idiot!' bellowed Faramond. 'Where were you?'

'Taking the cart over the river, as you told me to, Master.'

'Yolanda's curse, it set my feet a-fire.'

Winston stood on a chair and examined the soles of Faramond's feet. The skin was smooth and unblistered.

'Your feet are unharmed, Master.'

'Impossible! The agony was indescribable; they burned the soles off my boots and when I tried to walk, they burned footprints into the floorboards. The landlord fetched me a pail of water but my feet soon had it boiling.'

'Lady Yolantha said the curse comes to life when we're separated. Might it be that the curse burns anything in contact with the soles of your feet?'

Faramond appeared to be bursting a blood vessel. 'Obviously!'

'Did the pain stop when the landlord tied you upside down with your feet in the air?'

'Now that you mention it, yes.'

'So if your feet are bare and off the ground, you're not in pain?'

'Of course! Why else am I tied upside down from a roof beam?'

Winston broke off a piece of pie crust and held it against the sole of Faramond's right foot. It didn't burn, or even smoke.

'Master, now that I'm back, the curse is no longer active. We'll get you down.'

Faramond was gently lowered to the tavern floor by the landlord and other drinkers. His feet left no more charred imprints on the wooden floor, but the landlord wanted him out of the tavern as soon as possible.

Faramond's face faded from lurid red to merely ruddy. 'Dear me,' he groaned.

'Probably best not to get too far away from me from now on,' said Winston as they left the tavern. 'There's a cobbler's shop on the way to the ferry. We can get you another pair of boots.'

Once over the river, it was only another five miles to Kalderial. The moment Winston caught sight of Griffid, he knew there had been a change of attitude in the dragon. He was still curled up and asleep, but he was no longer overgrown with vines and bushes. He had shed a skin for the first time since Winston had known him, and the discarded skin lay in a crumpled heap as if Griffid had thrown it at an enormous laundry basket and missed. The not-quite-reptile looked younger and, more to the point, dangerous.

'Sneak past him, steal the jugs, leave a gold coin to replace them and flee quietly,' whispered Faramond as he and Winston crouched behind nearby bushes.

'But Master, the dragon no longer seems to be sleeping as deeply as in the past.'

'Just do as I say! I always know best.'

Winston was feeling vulnerable as he left the cover of the bushes. The impression of danger was heightened when Griffid opened his eyes, languidly stretched his neck and looked down at the apprentice.

'Griffid, how are you doing?' called Winston cheerily. 'You've given your scales a polish. Looking good, my scaley friend.'

What are you doing here? asked Griffid, as if talking to a guilty-looking dog trailing a string of sausages from its mouth.

'Payment for passage?' said Winston.

Travellers only pay when they want to leave the city by Summer Gate West. You are entering.

'Oh, ah, yes. Silly me.'

Without another word Griffid got to his feet, stretched his neck and reached over to the bushes behind Winston. There was a shriek of terror which ended abruptly. When the dragon withdrew his head to glare at Winston again, his cheeks were bulging.

'Is that who I think it is?' asked Winston.

The dragon nodded.

'I wouldn't swallow if I were you. Never know where he's been.'

Griffid opened his jaws and Faramond fell to the ground, covered in green saliva.

'It was the boy!' the wizard shouted. 'It was his idea to steal the jug.'

Look at my ears, said Griffid. *They're big, they can hear things a long way off. They heard you tell Winston to leave a gold coin for the jugs.*

'Well, er, yes. Value for money.'

I accept your offer. Toss the coin into my hoard.

Although surprised, Winston did as he was told.

Here are your jugs.

Griffid reached out with a claw midway along his wingtip and tapped at a puddle of silver on a flame-seared block of stone. It came loose with a faint clink. He tossed it to Winston.

I am being generous, he said as Winston picked up the disk of silver. *I melted both jugs together. The complete inscription is truly lost.*

'Er, did you read them?' Faramond asked.

Yes.

'Would you tell me the second one?'

Do I look stupid?

That sort of question from Winston would have drawn an absolutely predictable answer from Faramond, but the dragon had a body larger than the boat that had carried them from Loseros to Haldan, and breath that would've put the offshore volcano to shame.

'Dragons are said to be wiser than humans,' Winston managed diplomatically.

'Please, be reasonable,' said Faramond, who had not yet stirred from where he'd been dropped. 'The boy has been placed under a deadline curse. Under threat of mortal termination, he must find and present the two jugs to the elders of our order.'

He's holding them, replied Griffid.

'But you melted them. The inscriptions are gone.'

You can still see what's left of the handles on either side. Took real crafts-dragonship to get that effect.

'But Yolantha said—'

I know what Yolantha said – a little bird told me. Actually, it was a big black bird, perched at a window of the sanctum. Do you know what else she told me?

'I was there,' Faramond muttered.

Do you know what will happen to you, Winston?

'Something will eat me alive.'

The world is full of blind, invisible spirits. You can sometimes hear them howling on the wind. A deadline curse makes you attractive to them, and they are always hungry.

'Not to worry, lad, it will be over quickly,' said Faramond.

She also put a shackle curse on you, added Griffid. *Try to walk more than a hundred paces from Winston and the soles of your boots start to smoulder.*

'Griffid, you must have read the second inscription,' pleaded Faramond. 'Can't you tell us what it is?'

No.

'Don't you trust us?'

I don't trust the Guild Elders in general and Yolantha in particular.

'So the Yoal verse is something to do with the tower?'

It is something to do with a lot of things, and I am not telling you any of them. I like a quiet life, and if the Imperium Key leaves the tower, life will no longer be quiet. Will you be staying long in the city?

'If I'm to be eaten alive, does it matter where they lay the dining table?' said Winston.

Faramond turned out to be such a burden when Winston was hunting that he agreed to leave the wizard in the cart with his feet bare and dangling over the edge of the tray. Winston set up his web of cords to entangle whatever came down a narrow walkway in the undergrowth, fitted a spear blade to the end of his wayfarer's staff, and settled down in a tree to wait. Faramond had taken the magical staff that Yolantha had given the youth.

Winston sat idly toying with the chain around his neck, avoiding contact with the glass phial.

What was in there would regard even his sword as just a bit of extra crunchiness as she bolted Winston down . . . yet what was in there had stopped baring her fangs and snarling at him when he said she was beautiful. Is she actually beautiful? Winston wondered. She was basically a bat. Could bats be beautiful?

Against his better judgement, he lifted the phial out of his robe by the chain. The iffryt was so still that he thought she might have died. The claws on her wings that passed for her hands were about level with her head, and as Winston peered at her, she tapped against the glass with the claws of her left wing, while holding her right to her ear.

Glass, ear, Winston realised. Glass ear? No, he reasoned. More like hold the phial to his ear. Was that safe? Why not, the cork was in place.

'Winston, can you hear me?' said a tiny but clear voice.

'I hear you,' Winston replied.

'I know what Yolantha wants you to do. She thinks having an entrapped iffryt around your neck will fool the tower's spirit into thinking you are an iffryt too. She is wrong. You will be torn to pieces.'

Winston held the phial before his eyes for a moment. The little head nodded. He put the phial back to his ear.

'You want me to remove the cork,' he said. 'I've seen what you can do with the phial unstoppered.'

'Whatever you do, it's the same for me. Wear me on a chain as you enter the tower, and you die. Take me off before you enter, and you die. Flee deeper into the Harst Mountains and hide, you still die. Whatever happens, I remain trapped in this glass cage and I will fade over the years and centuries until I crumble.'

'The glass may break as I fall dead,' suggested Winston, who was not used to the idea of anyone being more miserable than himself.

'The glass phial is an extension of the tower. It cannot be broken, only unstoppered.'

'And whoever unstoppers it will be savagely killed.'

'Unless you know the control spells.'

'But I don't.'

'I could show them to you.'

'You could show me spells that don't work, and I could only test them by unstoppering the phial.'

'All true. So you will not unstopper the phial. I

have met hundreds like you over the millennia.'

Winston thought about this as he watched a panther walk down the trail, stare at the trap, then slink into the bushes beside the path and wait.

'Lady Yolantha wants me to perform a task that seems to have claimed more lives than a serious battle. Do what I will, and I die. Friendless and alone.'

'Like me,' replied Elvar.

'Were you free, what could you do?'

'There are free iffryts, I have heard Yolantha talking about them. They cannot escape back to our world through the portal, as it has been locked for three thousand years. Only energies flow through the portal.'

'Energies that allow you to perform incredible feats of enchantment, like transforming into a giant cat?'

'Yes.'

'But say you got into the tower, picked up the Imperium Key and did, well, something that Yolantha doesn't want you to. What then?'

'I would free every iffryt in this world and send them home.'

'You could do that?'

'I could.'

Winston thought carefully and decided that he had nothing to lose. He took a deep breath and cleared his throat.

'Why is lost but shall be found
See to my skip above the ground.
Find the room and find the ring
Win spell, win stone, win everything!'

For some moments, Elvar was silent with astonishment.

'They are the words?' she said in a voice almost choked with wonder. 'You knew them all along?'

'Aye.'

'Why did you not tell Yolantha?'

'Because I didn't trust her with them. She's a cruel person.'

Winston plucked the cork from the phial, hesitated for a moment, then flung it into the undergrowth below. He closed his eyes and waited for his arms to be torn from his body, his flesh ripped from his bones. Nothing happened. He opened his eyes. Elvar was still in the bottle.

'Why did you do that?' she asked. Her voice

was much easier to hear with the cork popped.

'Get out, do what you have to,' replied Winston.

'No. Tell me why you took the cork out and threw it away.'

'Because I want you out of the phial. Now go. Shoo! Go about your business.'

He turned the phial upside down and shook it. Elvar refused to come out.

'Is this some trick you arranged with Yolantha?' she asked.

'No.'

'Do you want to die?'

'I am going to die anyway. Fact. I would prefer to die for a good cause. Fact, also.'

'From what I have seen, a Countercast wizard would not know a good cause if it jumped out of his pie and bit him on the nose.'

'Faramond keeps telling me that I'll never be much of a Countercast wizard.'

Winston closed his eyes again. For a time, nothing happened, then something creaked. He opened his eyes. A girl of about his age was sitting on a nearby branch. She was dressed like Yolantha had been, and her hair was dark red and very long. Her skin was as pale as milk.

'Is that your real form?' asked Winston. By now, he knew that he was facing a very painful and unpleasant death, but was so sick of being manipulated and nagged that he was absolutely beyond caring.

'I took this form from your mind,' Elvar said. 'Is it a pleasing image?'

'I guess it is.'

'Few humans know what they really want; that is why my kind are bowled off their feet when such a person comes along.'

'So, you . . . want me to like you?'

'No, this is for me. I want to stop hating at least one human after three thousand years of slavery to humans and hating humans. I want to like you. I do hate you, yet here I am, trying not to.'

Winston wrinkled his forehead. 'I don't understand.'

'Nobody has ever uncorked that phial without a protective spell.'

'It must happen,' said Winston. 'Some iffryts escape.'

'Sometimes a wizard bungles the trace of the spell. The iffryt gets free and . . .'

'I don't need to know those details.'

'They then fly to Dracondas, to live out their time in the company of other escapees.'

'I notice that you're not flying east,' said Winston. 'I also notice that I'm still alive.'

'I haven't made up my mind about you. Perhaps I shall rip open your chest and eat your heart while it still beats . . . but not today.'

At that point a boar trotted into Winston's netting trap. He dropped to the ground, his improvised boar spear at the ready. Elvar strode forward, picked up the boar with one hand and flung it against the tree in which they had been sitting. The boar died instantly. The panther, which had been hiding nearby in the hope of stealing whatever Winston caught, fled.

'How was that, Master?' asked Elvar.

Winston put a hand to his forehead and closed his eyes while he got his thoughts in order. After eighteen months of calling Faramond 'Master', the idea of being someone else's master didn't hold any appeal for him.

'Two matters to clarify,' he said. 'I'm not your master.'

'As you wish.'

'And that gown is not suited to life on the road. Can you wear, say, the leathers of a journeyman tinker?'

'Nothing easier,' said Elvar, transforming the clothes instantly.

'Thank you. Do you like boar?'

'I'm sure I would.'

'Then you should eat what you have killed.'

'But Faramond expects to eat roast boar for dinner.'

'Roasting the boar will take hours, and we need to get back on the road as soon as possible. I shall tell him that there were no boars, and he will slap me and call me stupid. It's how I get my way.'

Soon after leaving the city, the spell maintaining the chicken hawk legs beneath the cart collapsed. The legs had been holding the cart eight feet off the road, and the wheels that the chicken legs had replaced reappeared. The cart fell eight feet. The impact of falling shattered all four wheels and both axles. Faramond had been in the cart at the time.

'I suppose we won't get the bond back on the sand cart now,' said Winston, as he collected the broken wood for a fire.

'We're on a Guild quest; I'll charge it to the Guild,' muttered Faramond, rubbing his backside.

'Do you really think Yolantha would pay?'

'That was a joke, stupid boy.'

They made camp amidst roadside trees. Hunting for dinner turned out to be easy. Winston strung his bow, aimed at the tree that they were sitting beneath, and shot an arrow into what Faramond thought was just a clump of leaves. There was a brief squawk, and a crow impaled by an arrow fell to the ground.

'Dinner is on the way,' said Winston.

'That might have been Morach!' exclaimed the horrified Faramond.

'She's a raven and that's a crow.'

Faramond waved a hand. 'I don't have my *What Bird is That?* scroll to hand.'

'Trust me, Master, it's a crow, but if it makes you feel any better, it was probably also a spy for the dragon. We now have an hour or so to talk freely before Griffid sends another bird.'

'Talk freely?' sighed Faramond. 'What can we possibly have to talk about? You are going to be eaten by demons of the air, and if that happens, I will have to crawl about on my hands and knees with my feet bare. Forever.'

'Only until you die, Master.'

'*That* does not comfort me.'

'Now we have privacy,' said Winston as he unpacked the splash of silver that Griffid had given him. He held it up by what was left of the handles.

'*Find the room and find the ring*,' he began.

'The inscription!' exclaimed Faramond, snatching the silver mess from Winston and staring at it. His eyes squinted. 'Wait a moment. There's no inscription.'

'Not any more. When I added our jug to the six others in Griffid's hoard, I happened to notice that one of them had a couple of lines engraved on the side.'

'You devious wretch! Why didn't you tell Yolantha and the elders that you memorised the full spell?'

'How long do you think they would have let us live? People with secret, powerful spells like to keep them secret. You saw how easily she killed one of her own wizards.'

'I've taught you well, young Winston,' Faramond said grudgingly. 'Never trust anyone.'

'Good advice, Master.'

'But why didn't you tell me?'

'I never trust anyone, Master.'

Once the crow had been reduced to bones and feathers, Winston cleaned the arrow that he had shot it with and returned it to his quiver.

'Well?' asked Faramond impatiently. 'Last line?'

'Win spell, win stone, win everything!'

'By the Odd Gods, a riddle!' said Faramond. 'Win spell, win stone. *Winston Spellwyn.* Your name!'

'That's unlikely, Master. The lines are three thousand years old. I'm fourteen.'

'A prophecy, then. Dare I say it, but perhaps you alone of all wizards might be able to enter the Blackstone Tower. Of course, that would exclude myself.'

'So, someone knew about me back then?'

'It seems so. Some scruffy old prophet sitting in a cave back then spied on you doing your infernal experiments, and paid a tinsmith to scratch your name onto a jug. It sounds strange, but I've seen stranger things.'

'Why, Master?' asked Winston.

'To give you an advantage. The Blackstone Tower is well defended. Heroes, armies, wizards – even dragons have not been able to break in.'

'I heard that a lot of them broke in easily enough. Getting out was the hard part.'

'Don't you contradict me, wretched boy.'

'Er, Master?' said Winston, peering into the distance.

'What now?'

'You know how I said Griffid would send another crow to spy on us?'

'Yes, and what of it?'

'He's decided not to bother with the crow.'

Winston had never seen the dragon so angry. Tendrils of smoke curled around his mouth, and even Morach the raven hovered well clear of him.

'Griffid, how are you doing?' called Winston as he stood to greet him.

Faramond was already hiding behind a tree.

I am a master of deduction, declared the dragon. *You came out here, well beyond the range of even my sensitive hearing. You then shot my little bird.*

'We were hungry,' said Winston.

You shot it to hide words from me. Were they words about the Lost Spell of Yoal?

'Trust me, mighty Griffid, I—'

Why did you kill my listener bird?

'As you can see, we were hungry and it was within bowshot.'

Very droll, but Morach and I are quite fond of flame-grilled wizard. You two have the power to breach the tower, Winston. I cannot allow that.

Griffid drew breath, opening his jaws. Winston dived for the cover of some fallen stonework, tripped, and fell headlong. This is the end, he thought. Maybe it'll be so quick that it won't hurt much.

A massive black cat, comparable in size to Griffid, materialised beside the continent's youngest wizard. The dragon drew another breath and poured a torrent of fire down over the campsite and trees. Winston was not at all sure what was protecting him from the flames, but he was fairly certain that they were being deflected, because nothing hurt. The cat now opened its mouth and seared the dragon with its own flaming breath. Although dragons are proof against destruction by fire, it's only in the same way that humans are proof against a solid punch. In both cases it's not fatal but it hurts a great deal. Griffid nearly fell over himself as he scrambled back, then lumbered away to gain speed. He finally became airborne.

'I am alive!' Faramond chortled behind Winston. 'Never underestimate the power of a Countercast magician, m'boy!'

Faramond was sitting behind the charred stump of the tree that had initially protected him. He stood, hands spread wide as though encompassing the world.

'Allow me to introduce you to Elvar,' said Winston. 'She's an iffryt.'

Faramond blinked, then stared up at the enormous black feline face. His mouth gaped.

Elvar replied with what might have been a purr but was probably a growl.

'I freed her,' Winston added.

'You freed an iffryt? What a stupid . . .'

Elvar glared at him and hissed.

'What a stupid situation to find ourselves in. The tent, our money, everything's been burned except the clothes we stand in.'

'I still have my purse, and there's a wayfarer's inn about five miles to the west,' said Winston.

'Five miles!' exclaimed Faramond. 'You can't expect me to walk five miles. I'm not moving until there's something to carry me.' As an afterthought, he added, 'Pleased to make your acquaintance, um, Elvar.'

'The Blackstone Tower is three hundred miles to the west, deep in the Harst Mountains,' said Winston, looking at a map he kept within his robe. 'Elvar, can you take us there?'

He turned to face Elvar, but she was once more in her human form. Faramond shrieked, then figured that there was probably nothing to be alarmed about.

'Tonight, we stay at the inn,' she said. 'In the morning we shall begin our journey.'

'Journey?' exclaimed Faramond.

'To the Blackstone Tower.'

'That's three hundred miles.'

'By road.'

'You expect me to walk *three hundred miles*?'

'Oh no, I will do the walking.'

'As the cat?'

'Meow. Meantime, you will walk the five miles to the wayfarer's tavern.'

Faramond opened his mouth to shout her down, but just in time managed to remind himself that she could manifest as something that made even Griffid realise that he had more important business elsewhere.

'Come on, the sooner we reach the wayfarer's inn, the sooner we can have dinner,' he muttered as he shambled off.

The following morning, once they were out of sight of the wayfarer's inn, Elvar gave them the rules for travelling with her. Faramond tried to protest, but the alternative was walking, so he soon conceded defeat. Winston rode on her back, holding onto her thick, silky fur. Elvar padded along with Faramond dangling by his trail cloak, which she held in her teeth.

'Will the entire journey be like this?' he called as they travelled beside the Harst River, much to the alarm of other travellers on the road.

'Remember, Master, she refuses to have your bottom sitting on her fur,' called Winston.

'But even at this pace it will be three whole days!'

'Can't be helped, Master.'

Chapter Five

The ancient pinnacle known as Blackstone Mountain thrust upwards like a long, straight thorn, in such a remote area of the Harst Mountains that even goatherds didn't bother taking their flocks to graze there. Most of the time Elvar followed the river, and every so often she dunked Faramond in the water. Eventually, he got the hint and took to washing his clothes each night, drying them by the campfire.

They reached the tower at the end of their third day of travelling, just as the sun was setting behind the surrounding mountains. The tower was about a mile from where they made camp, but even at that distance they could see that reaching the front door was going to be a challenge.

'A thousand feet high,' sighed Faramond. 'No wonder nobody can break in. You need to be a mountain climber as well as a wizard.'

'The tower is built on a small but thin mountain, like a needle made of rock,' said Winston, making a more detailed assessment of it. 'Only the top two hundred feet are tower. Look carefully, you can just make out a spiral stairway winding around the mountain.'

'That's still eight hundred feet of climbing,' said Faramond. 'I'm not suited to the mountaineering life.'

'You mean you're shorter than Winston, yet you weigh three hundred pounds,' said Elvar, who once again was in human form.

'What you call fat is my magical reserve.'

'*You* are afraid to approach the tower,' insisted Elvar.

'No, I'm not.' Faramond pulled his shoulders back and straightened his robe. 'I'm just more of an academic wizard than a warrior.'

'The path is probably built for human feet, Elvar,' observed Winston, hoping to change the direction of the exchange before it became a deadly argument. 'Do you still want to enter it with me?'

'It is my destiny to enter it,' she replied.

The sun was down, the fire was reduced to coals, and Faramond was snoring by the time Elvar spoke again. She and Winston were sitting together, wrapped in their blankets and crouched down out of the icy mountain winds.

'Winston, do you trust me?' Elvar asked.

'You haven't eaten me yet, so yes, I suppose I do.'

'Why? Yolantha is rich and powerful. Retrieve the Imperium Key for her, and she might indeed let you live and endorse your entry to the Guild.'

'I know, I know,' Winston said. 'And if I don't retrieve the amulet, I'll probably end up living in a pond and wondering where my next fly is coming from. What do you think our chances are?'

Elvar's face hardened. 'Venture into that tower without me, and you will be killed, like the apprentice who stole the Imperium Key all those years ago. Together, we can liberate an entire world from slavery.'

Winston's eyes widened. '*A* world? Your world?'

'*My* world, Winston.'

'And then what?'

'I just vanish from your life.'

Winston shook his head. 'A life that Yolantha will be trying to end.'

'Trust me, Winston, Yolantha's powers will be no greater than yours if you get me into the tower.'

Leaving Faramond at their camp with his bare feet propped on a rock, Winston and Elvar set off to walk the last mile to the tower.

'Hand in hand,' said Elvar, grasping Winston's hand.

'Your hand!' he exclaimed as their fingers intertwined. 'It's like you have a raging fever.'

'For me, that's normal. The iffryt of the tower sees us even now. So long as we are in contact, he will think we are just one iffryt.'

'Ah. And what about Faramond? I mean, I'd rather not return to the camp and find just a few well-gnawed bones.'

'The spell on his feet is iffryt magic, so he may look like some iffryt's captive and be ignored.'

'May?'

'I don't know everything.'

Upon reaching the base of the little mountain, Winston saw bones and armour scattered here and there.

'Heroes who fell from the steps?' asked Winston.

'Heroes who were pushed,' replied Elvar. 'Those who reached the door of the tower flew there on dragons, enchanted carpets or levitation castings. If we reach the door by the steps, we may be the first to do so in three thousand years.'

They began the long ascent of the spiral path. There was no handrail, and the wind was so blustery that Winston wondered if it was some invisible spirit trying to blow them off the side of the mountain. Every hundred steps they passed a stone gargoyle with golden jewels for eyes. Each gargoyle was seven feet tall, and their eyes followed them as they passed.

'Surely they see that I'm not an iffryt,' said Winston.

'They are extensions of the tower's iffryt, and not very bright. They see me attached to you, and the tower's iffryt does not hate other iffryts. Nine iffryts have escaped their phials in recorded history, so the tower's original master, Lord Cabal, wove defences to destroy any iffryt that tried to breach it.'

'So the tower kills iffryts as well as humans?'

'Yes.'

'But holding hands confuses both defences.'

'Apparently.'

'Apparently?' gasped Winston, holding up their tightly clasped hands. 'You mean this is just a guess?'

'Yes, but it is a good guess.'

'We might've been killed by now!'

'And you might have been killed when you drew the stopper from my phial and threw it away. Sometimes we have no choice but to gamble.'

'Gambling should always be a last resort. My mother always said that gamblers end up ruined or dead.'

'Gamble sparingly. I do.'

Back at the camp, Faramond had a problem. More specifically, he had nine problems, and all of them were wolves. He lay on his back with his feet in the air, unable to run, not that he could have outrun a wolf under any circumstances. The wolves sensed that he was helpless, but not why.

At first Faramond managed to keep them from closing in by flinging bits of burning wood from the campfire at them. This worked until the wizard ran out of burning wood. The alpha wolf approached for the kill, radiating confidence and malice. Faramond tried tracing a spell, but nothing happened. The curse on his feet was interfering with his magical powers.

'Why me and not Winston?' he mumbled, then realised the truth almost straight away. Winston was under a different curse, one that required almost no power because it had not yet become active. Yolantha had known that Winston did all the work, and needed to trace spells and do castings.

Faramond kicked at the wolf, but it wasn't intimidated. The leg of its prey was just something to bite. It seized Faramond's foot, and Yolantha's spell guaranteed that this was roughly the same as biting a red-hot iron bar. The wolf yelped, tripped over itself as it made a frantic, scrambling turn, then bolted away, whining in pain and no longer the alpha wolf.

The beta wolf now stepped forward, but Faramond had by now realised that his feet were actually potent weapons. The beta wolf leapt, Faramond kicked at it, and the animal ran away yelping with its fur trailing smoke. Faramond had singed the gamma and delta wolves and sent them on their way before the remaining five wolves decided that a mountain goat would be a lot less trouble than this human.

Faramond now had to crawl about on his hands and knees to gather the scattered firewood, but as he was no longer in danger of being eaten, he was *almost* in a good mood.

By counting his steps, Winston estimated that the spiral path would have been two miles long if stretched out straight.

'Faramond was right, he would have had a heart attack before the halfway marker,' panted Winston to Elvar. Begrudgingly, he observed, 'You're not even wheezing.'

'Iffryts don't get tired,' said Elvar. 'Not here,

anyway. My world is close and I feel its energies. I can even smell them.'

Winston sniffed the air. While far cleaner than the air of Loseros or Haldan, it was not the typical mountain air they had been breathing for the past few days. The scents here were like nothing Winston had ever encountered. The portal to an alien world was very close.

'Were we in danger last night?' he asked.

'Yes and no. A lot of strange things were prowling about near the camp, but they were not inclined to approach with me there.'

'Things? From the tower?'

'Things that are bound to the tower. Extensions of the tower. Visitors are not welcome hereabouts.'

'Were they dangerous?'

'You mean to people? Yes.'

Winston fingered the pommel of his sword, then felt for his knife.

'Are you a hero, with biceps the size of bread loaves?' asked Elvar.

'I'm more of a scholar who travels a bit and knows how to avoid trouble. Being around

Faramond has taught me to keep my head down.'

'Then don't bother with weapons. Yolantha showed you what happened to heroes who snuck into the tower.'

'How did she do that? How did she see in there?'

'She didn't. The very oldest chronicles describe the interior, from back in the days when it was safe for visitors. She knows from the chronicles how many entered the tower in search of the Imperium Key, and who they were. All she did was imagine their bones on the floor.'

'I've been able to learn very little about the apprentice who stole the Imperium Key and tried to close the portal,' Winston admitted.

'That is because very little is known about him.'

'Why'd he do it? Did he think it was cruel to treat iffryts like lumps of coal? Sources of power and nothing else?'

'Nobody knows, nobody living, anyway. Yolantha thinks he was from another guild of wizardry; one whose master resented the sheer power that the Summoners could wield.'

'That could be any of them.'

'True.'

Winston thought about this as they climbed. There were more guilds of wizardry than he had fingers on his hands but only the members of the Countercasts' Guild ate like food was about to go out of fashion. The Recallectants forgot the spells once they cast them, so they spent most of their time in libraries re-learning the spells. The Amulans carried dragon eggs and drew upon their power. There were not many of these, because the dragons were rather sensitive about having their eggs stolen. The Summoners were princes among wizards because they stole their power from captive iffryts. They were impossible to defeat, so there were always plots to destroy the portal to the iffryt world.

'Yolantha's a rogue Summoner, however, so she probably knows about weaknesses that others didn't,' ventured Winston.

'I only heard what she spoke when I was worn around her neck, Winston. She must have plans for when she gets hold of the Imperium Key, but I do not know them.'

'So what should I do with it?'

'That will depend on what we find inside the tower.'

'The door's not far now,' he said, searching for a less dangerous topic. 'I'm amazed that we got all the way up the steps without anything trying to kill us.'

'I told you, we look like neither iffryt nor human, but have a suggestion of both.'

'Getting in is sure to be a problem,' sighed Winston, who had decided that life was just a collection of problems strung out between cradle and grave.

'That is not how it works with magical places. Getting out again is always far more difficult.'

Winston tilted his head. 'And on the subject of the tower, just what do we do once we're inside?'

'Find the Imperium Key, I suppose.'

'And then?'

'Hopefully, it will be obvious.'

'You're gambling again,' muttered Winston.

'Once again, it is a last resort,' replied Elvar.

Even the wolves had not caused Faramond as much terror as the sight of Yolantha's head appearing in the flames of his fire.

Her eyebrows rose. 'Surprised?'

'No, I mean, that is, yes,' Faramond stuttered.

'I can follow you by the curse on your feet. Where are you?'

'Nearing the tower, Ladyship, and all is well.'

The head in the flames turned, and Yolantha saw that Blackstone Tower was indeed visible in the distance.

'Where is Winston?'

'Away, hunting. I fancied a bite of fresh, roast rabbit before approaching the tower.'

'You put your stomach before recovering the Imperium Key?' she shouted.

'Well . . . that is . . . yes and no,' Faramond spluttered. 'I mean, no, most certainly not! But . . . the lad is also scouting the land around the mountain and its tower, looking for sentry spells. Yes, that's what he's doing.'

Yolantha's face contorted as she fought down her fury.

'Well then, seeing you are so fond of the local wildlife, why don't I call some to you.'

The sorceress threw back her head and made a call that was more of a bellow than a howl.

Faramond wasn't familiar with whatever it was, but it sounded disturbing.

'That is the call of a female mountain bear,' she said. 'Very soon you will have all the male mountain bears that you can eat.'

Yolantha's face vanished from the flames. Somewhere in the distance came the answering call of a mountain bear. Then another. And another. Soon, they echoed all around him.

When they finally reached the door, Winston saw that it was also studded with brass nails in the shape of eyes. Each eye was inset with a different type of gemstone, and there were more eyes than he could count.

'So now we knock?' asked Winston.

'Bad idea,' replied Elvar.

'Why? I like to try the easy way first.'

'You know what the demon of this tower is sure to hate?' asked Elvar.

'You'd better tell me,' said Winston.

'Visitors. Knights on quests, looking for something interesting to kill. Goatherds wanting to be turned into princes or princesses. Wizards wanting to trade a bag of gold for a year's supply of magical power. Then there are tourist guides wanting to pose with their customers for a group sketch portrait, and don't get me started on priests who want to do exorcisms. You're different.'

'I suppose even monsters appreciate good manners.'

'True, and your manners are very good. I do believe that I no longer hate you, alone out of all humans.'

Winston suddenly felt a stab of alarm. The iffryt liked him. He reminded himself that he was holding hands with something big and powerful enough to send a dragon scampering. As far as Winston was concerned, Elvar was his perfect girl, yet she had made herself look that way. He reminded himself that he was eight hundred feet up a mountain capped by a tower formed out of a living iffryt. Apparently, it was in a bad mood after being trapped there for three thousand years. Yes, he was holding hands with an attractive girl, but no, she wasn't the girl from the hovel next door; she wasn't even a human. There was no point even thinking romantic thoughts.

Diplomatically, Winston shook his head. 'I've

never thought of you as a monster,' was the best reply he could think of.

'And I don't think of you as human.'

'You don't?'

'Humans are hateful. Weeks ago, when Yolantha showed me to you, you said I was pretty. That was the first compliment I have been given since the portal tore me out of my home world. Winston of Shop Spellwyn, you said something nice to me. You are not like other humans. That is the only reason you are still alive.'

It was a relief that she didn't wish to get married in the next temple they arrived at, then settle down in a nice little cottage to live happily ever after, yet Winston wondered what she really meant. Maybe their chances of getting out of this alive were zero, and she just wanted to cheer him up a bit first.

Winston concentrated on the huge and forbidding pair of doors studded with hundreds of eyes. Could any of them see? Could *all* of them see? This didn't seem like a good place for indecision. Something that was sure to be watching might conclude that they were human and iffryt.

'The doors should be easy to open, you say?' he asked.

'Easy.'

Easy? Winston wondered. As easy as chanting a few words of verse? He cleared his throat.

'Why is lost but shall be found
See to my skip above the ground.'

The doors gave a loud groan, as if being woken from a long and pleasant sleep and being very annoyed about it. They swung inwards. That was too easy, thought Winston. Easy was another word for trap.

'Come along, and hold on to my hand at all times,' said Elvar, when Winston showed no signs of taking the first step. 'Never, *never* let go. Understand?'

'I don't understand, but I'll hold tight.'

Together they stepped into the darkness. The doors shut behind them with a shattering boom, like thunder from a storm that had nearly arrived overhead. As they crept along, a light appeared from nowhere in particular, growing in intensity until the interior of the tower was illuminated as brightly as daylight.

As far as Winston could make out, stairs surrounded a central space littered with bones, but it was not quite the same as he had seen in Yolantha's vision. Winston was particularly surprised by what appeared to be the remains of a knight in plate armour and chainmail, holding a lance. He was astride the skeleton of a fallen horse. How did someone get all that up here? Winston wondered.

Two skeletons lay near the lowest of the stairs, and Winston and Elvar went down on their knees to inspect them more closely. One was that of a child, the blade of a sword in his ribs. Close behind the child was a man. His bones were not in any sort of armour, although jewelled rings were on his fingers. His bones had been crushed so flat they were no thicker than expensive parchment.

'Lord Cabal and the rogue apprentice,' said Elvar. 'Now we know their fate.'

'You might, I don't,' said Winston.

'The key protects the wearer, Winston. This boy was holding the key, not wearing it, so Lord Cabal was able to put a sword through his heart. Then, because Cabal didn't snatch up the key at once, there was a moment when the key had no human master. Lord Cabal was smashed flat in that moment.'

'Apparently, by a fist at least two yards across,' added Winston. He anxiously glanced upwards.

'And there is the Imperium Key,' said Elvar. 'Pick it up.'

No dust, Winston thought as he removed the key and chain from the small, skeletal fingers. No dust meant something cleansed the place. Demonic servants? He and Elvar hadn't wiped their feet before entering. Did the servants get angry when visitors with dusty feet walked on their nice clean stairs?

'Should I put the key on?' asked Winston.

'Probably a good idea.'

'*Probably*? Are we doing the gambling thing again? Lady Fortune doesn't like people who get too familiar with her.'

'Too many questions, Winston. This very brave youth was charged with doing what you are about to attempt. Keep hold of my hand.

The tower iffryt probably knows we are here to help.'

'Probably.'

'Enough talk. Time to show you what is at the top of the stairs.'

'You know already?'

'There is a very old chronicle with descriptions. Yolantha paid a fortune for her copy. The Summoner wizards had all the others destroyed.'

Winston looked up again before putting his foot on the first step. The blocks in the domed ceiling progressively overlapped each other, and the weight of the entire dome held the stones in place. It was a common enough design in big buildings. Take away the keystone and the whole lot would come tumbling down. The air felt moist, but that was probably because it was so cold. The walls, the bones, the broken weapons and armour, all were quite dry.

'This is like the cold, cloying dead air of a long-forgotten sepulchre,' said Winston as they climbed. 'There are plenty of those in Kalderial.'

'This place is many things,' said Elvar. 'Sepulchre, battlefield, machine, gateway and living guard. All of these stones are alive, so don't spit or do anything else untoward.'

The stairs led to a gallery surrounding the disk of black nothingness, and once they were inside it, they saw that it supported an arch of interlocking stones between the disk and the dome of the roof.

'What now?' asked Winston.

'We climb the stairs of that arch.'

'I knew you were going to say that. Those stairs are only about a foot wide. How do we climb them while still holding hands?'

'With extreme care. Come along.'

At the apex of the arch was a stone platform, and half embedded in this was a great black ring, two yards in diameter. Winston suspected that it had once been polished silver, but black tarnish now covered it entirely. Exactly below it was a slit that was about the right size and shape for the Imperium Key.

'I'm open to suggestions,' said Winston.

'Chant the last two lines of the verse.'

'*Find the room and find the ring*

Win stone, win spell, win everything!'

Nothing happened.

'I'm Winston Spellwyn,' he called.

Again, nothing happened.

'The lines may be instructions, not a spell,' said

Elvar. 'I think you have to do something with the ring and key.'

'Like what? The ring's huge, I can't wear it.'

'Try turning it.'

'It's set in the platform, and the platform's solid rock. I can't even see the bottom half.'

'Well, just staring at it won't do anything, and there *is* a keyhole.'

Winston took the key from his neck, put it into the slot and turned. There was a dull clunk from within the platform. He withdrew the key and placed it around his neck again. He peered over the edge. The disk of absolute nothingness floated beneath him, unchanged.

'Winston, you're putting off what comes next,' said Elvar.

'What's that?'

'The ring. We need to turn the *ring*.'

'How? It's *still* embedded in solid stone.'

Elvar pointed.

Winston looked up. Engraved in the metal was the spell for *locked*.

'So on the other side of the ring is another spell saying unlocked?'

'Perhaps. Grasp the ring with me and push.'

Together they pushed with their free hands. The ring didn't move. They went around to the other side and pushed. This time the ring moved smoothly. Gleaming metal, free of tarnish, rose free of the stone.

'I see another spell,' gasped Winston. 'It says *unlocked*.'

'Keep turning it.'

As the ring turned, the spell rose higher and higher. When it reached the apex there was another clunk.

'It's unlocked,' said Winston. 'What now?'

'Look over the edge.'

Winston looked. The disk of nothingness was falling, and as it touched the floor it opened up to a vast shaft that reached straight down into the depths of the mountain. Black dust rained down all around them.

'The dome, it's dissolving!' cried Winston.

'The iffryt of the tower is escaping!' Elvar shouted back. 'Hold on to me and grip the ring with your other hand.'

Looking up, Winston saw that the dome had

dissolved, and red streaks were dropping in from the sky, things that were just blurs that shot past and vanished into the pit of blackness that the floor of the tower had become. They generated a wind as strong as a winter gale.

'What's happening?' shouted Winston above the rushing air.

'The tower is a portal that allows energies to flow in from my world. Before the Imperium Key was lost, it also allowed the keeper of the key to draw iffryts out of my world like a human fishing in a stream.'

'But the red things are leaving our world.'

'Yes, we unlocked the portal. They're iffryts, escaping their human wizards, the Summoners. Phials will be bursting all over your world as they escape.'

'What about us? What happens if we let go of the ring?'

'We both get drawn into my world. You wouldn't last long.'

'Let me get this straight. I'm to die when your hand gets tired?'

'Maybe not. Just . . . try to stay calm.'

'*Stay calm*? Why should I worry about not soiling my trousers as I'm falling to my death?'

'Because we may be able to fly.'

'*Fly*? Is this another of your gambles?'

'Winston, swear yourself into my service.'

'What? I'm sure to die within the next minute, yet you want me bound to you?'

'Don't argue, just swear it!'

'I swear.'

Winston was aware of a tingling feeling in his right hand. When he dared to look down, he saw that it had vanished, and that his arm was getting shorter and vanishing into Elvar's hand. His upper arm, then shoulder, soon followed.

'Is this supposed to be happening?' he cried.

'I think so. I've never done it before.'

'Has anyone?'

'Not that I know of.'

Winston had the impression that he was falling as his head was absorbed by her fingers, then there was blackness. For a moment he felt totally calm and at peace, but he was fairly sure that it wouldn't last.

Faramond had thought his problems were over when the third mountain bear had lumbered away, its nose burned and its fur smoking. Then Blackstone Tower collapsed down to its foundations. Was that supposed to happen? he wondered. Wretched boy, caused me nothing but grief.

All at once Faramond realised that if Yolantha's head reappeared in the flames, she only had to turn around to see that the tower was gone. He had no idea if that was good or bad. Why couldn't people leave him alone to be a hermit wizard?

What Faramond might have lacked in competence, he made up in cunning. It took only moments for him to snatch up his water skin and douse the flames. He now had nothing to drink and no fire to keep him warm, but when compared to explaining to Yolantha why he'd sent Winston to the tower while he remained in their camp beside the fire, the discomforts were barely noticeable.

Winston's eyes opened sluggishly, and he saw that he was flying around the edge of the infinitely deep chasm, fighting the wind that was pouring into it. The sides of the tower were streamers of black dust that became red as they fell. The arch with the ring remained, like a frail skeleton of the structure. Suddenly, Winston realised what was wrong with his hands. His thumb and two of his fingers had grown short claws, but the other two had become enormous and fully formed wings.

'Pay attention, the good part is coming!' shouted Winston's lips.

Did I say that? he wondered. He was fairly sure that he hadn't.

The red streaks had ceased streaming into the portal, the tower had dissolved, and even the gargoyles that had been stationed on the stairs spiralling up Blackstone Mountain were lumbering up to the peak and leaping into the disk – or more accurately – chasm. Finally, the arch collapsed, falling into the portal which then vanished instantly; the peak of the mountain then healed over.

Winston now concentrated on himself. He couldn't turn his head, but what he could see out of the corners of his eyes made him scream with terror.

'Calm yourself,' said Elvar's voice through his own lips. 'You can have your true form back when we land.'

What have you done to me? Winston cried, but the words only sounded in his mind, in the way that Griffid's voice had.

'I've given you my natural form,' explained Elvar, and this time the words had real sound.

But you're an iffryt.

'And iffryts can fly in their true form. Right now, we need to be able to fly. The ground is a long way down.'

The moment they landed, Elvar morphed their common body back into Winston.

'I'm alive,' he said, patting at himself, mildly surprised that his clothes had been returned to him as well.

You're alive, you're human, and you have not even soiled your trousers, said Elvar in Winston's mind.

'And you're talking mindspeak.'

It's the only way I can talk when you are in your own body.

'So I can't control my body when I'm, well, you?'

No.

Winston lifted the Imperium Key from his neck and dropped it into a sleeve of his robe.

If you wear that on your neck, nothing can harm you, Elvar pointed out.

'If Yolantha sees me wearing it, she might think I'm getting ideas above my station, and not lift the deadline curse from me. Will the Imperium Key protect me from that?'

I have not studied the theory of such curses. Her curse was cast before you put the key on, so it may be like a sword wound. It happened before you started *wearing the key, so it doesn't get healed.*

'In that case, why bother wearing it?'

Suit yourself.

'And what about becoming you?'

That must be an act of will by whichever of us holds the body's form.

'Right. I can only become you if I do whatever I have to do, and the same for you becoming me?'

Yes, but there is one little problem.

'There always is,' Winston mumbled.

There is no more portal, so there is no more power coming in from my world. If you want to morph into me, and whenever I morph into you, it will come out of your body's resources.

'You call that a *little* problem?' exclaimed Winston.

It will remain little as long as we do not morph too often.

Winston tried to stand up, realised that he was as tired as if he had just done a sixteen-hour hike, and hurriedly sat down. He stood again, more slowly this time. His head spun for some moments before he felt steady enough to walk. Then he set off for the campsite.

I imagine this is what it is like to be male, said Elvar in Winston's mind. *The balance is slightly different. Narrower hips, perhaps.*

'Haven't you morphed into male humans . . . and other things?'

There are different sorts of morphing. Girl iffryts morph into girls. Same for boys. Now I share a body made up from the substances of this world, and they have different properties.

Winston thought very carefully before speaking again.

'Look, about what happened?'

Yes?

'You could have just dived into the portal.'

I could have.

'Yet you didn't.'

Winston, if I had abandoned you directly above the portal, what do you think would have happened?

'I would've fallen into your world.'

And died. If I had morphed into my true form and flown you clear of the portal, then released you and flown back, what would have happened?

'I . . . was about eight hundred feet up.'

Enough said. I did not have time to fly you down to solid rock and return to the portal before it collapsed.

'Oh. Thank you, but . . .'

But why did I merge with your body?

'That was indeed going to be the next question.'

Once the portal closed, the energies from my world would be cut off. I would disperse like smoke on the wind. Die, in other words. Yes, I saved you, but I did extract a price.

'You could've just left me. Like Faramond would have.'

I could not have done that – it was a matter of honour.

You saved thousands of my kind, and changed your own world forever.

'Well yes, I suppose that much is true,' sighed Winston, suddenly realising how many important and powerful people would be angry with him. 'All over the place there will be Summoner wizards looking for honest work or joining the Countercasters and looking for a good cook. What about the Imperium Key?'

It is still dangerous, even with the portal closed. Yolantha can wear it to avoid assassination – there will probably be a lot of assassins being sent after her now. Winston, we will be travelling back into a very different world. What do you want to do in it?

'My mother taught me lots of things about herbs, and I watched as she lanced boils and cleaned wounds. I wasn't allowed to watch babies being born, but midwives usually do that sort of thing.'

You are saying that people are always getting sick, so there will be work for you as a physician?

'Yes.'

You will not return to magic?

'No – but it might be fun to morph into your

form and let you fly about. Is it important to fly, like in your world?'

Yes. Where I come from there is a red sun that never sets, and there are other things about it that your language has no words for. One side is too hot for life and the other is too cold. There is only a narrow band around the middle where my kind may live. We have very strange powers and needs . . . but like I said, there are no words in your language to describe them.

'How long will you, like, share my body?'

Always.

'What? I've become half a girl?'

You're totally male, but if Faramond pushes you into a chasm on the way home, we can transform into me again and fly.

'And you, can't you become a male bat – iffryt – thing?'

I told you, the enchantment does not work that way. Besides, why would I want to be male?

'You're male now.'

No, I am not. I am just in your body for the ride.

'But you can see and hear everything I do?'

Yes. Be on your best behaviour, Winston!

Chapter Six

Faramond was alive but alarmed when Winston reached the camp. He'd seen the tower collapse and thought Winston and Elvar both dead, but Winston told him that Elvar had escaped into some sort of magic portal. Due to the curse on his feet, he'd been facing the prospect of returning to civilisation on his hands and knees, so alarm changed to happiness. As they walked, Winston described what he'd seen inside the tower, but not what he'd done to destroy the portal.

Faramond frowned. 'But you've not told me why the tower collapsed and vanished.'

'It may've had something to do with removing the Imperium Key from it.'

'But the tower existed when the Summoners kept the key in distant Varlin.'

'Master, I'm only a provisional wizard. All I can tell you is that I walked out of the tower and it collapsed into an infinitely deep well.'

Faramond looked up sharply. 'You have the Imperium Key?'

'I put it in my pack.'

Once they'd made their camp, Winston said he had to go hunting while the sun was still up. Leaving Faramond on his back with his bare feet propped up, he set off to hunt. Winston was some distance away from the campsite when Elvar spoke in his mind.

Why don't I do the hunting, Winston? I can see in the dark.

'No!'

Why not?

'Call me old-fashioned, but when I go hunting, I'd rather not use three-inch talons to catch dinner,' Winston grumbled. 'Besides, I'm still exhausted from that transformation out of your natural form this morning.'

I must admit that I am shocked by the human feeling of tiredness. How do you live with it?

'With patience, careful management, and a lot of sleep.' Winston stifled a yawn. 'How do I morph back into you if there's an emergency and I need to fly?'

Trace the spell for iffryt and clap once.

'Then spend the next fortnight recovering?'

That too.

Within an hour Winston had speared three trout in the river and with his bow and arrow had shot a young mountain goat. Back at the camp, he gave Faramond a few instructions about butchering and spit roasting, then lay back and fell asleep, too exhausted to even dream.

Elsewhere in the world, many hundreds of Summoner wizards had discovered that the iffryts that had provided their powers had escaped. Some were thinking about getting mundane jobs, while others were wondering whether to switch to a different magical guild and re-train. All – those who hadn't been horrifically slain by their iffryts – were wondering who might have been responsible for the magical catastrophe, and were plotting revenge.

Winston jerked awake, astounded to see Yolantha of Yoal's face amid the flickering flames of the campfire. She was glaring at Faramond. Winston realised that he was unfamiliar with this sort of magic.

'Explain what just happened, Faramond!' she said, with a dangerous edge to her voice. 'Messenger birds have been arriving all day. A dozen Summoner wizards have reported that their slave iffryts have escaped, and dozens more probably sent birds that are still on the way.'

'We – ah, that is – I recovered the Imperium Key.'

Faramond held up the key that Winston had brought back from the tower.

Winston glowered.

'Guard it with your life or I shall take your life,' snarled Yolantha, who didn't seem at all impressed by the feat. 'What about the tower?'

'It, ah, collapsed when I left. With the key, that is.'

'Why would it do that?'

'I can't say. It just did.'

Winston was about to call out that Faramond had never been within a mile of the tower when he realised that the wizard was doing him a great favour. A lot of people would be very angry about the tower vanishing and the portal sealing itself shut. It was far better to leave the credit, glory, blame and consequences with Faramond.

Winston groaned, and Yolantha's image instantly turned on him.

'Winston!' she snapped. 'Give *your* account of how the tower came to collapse.'

'I can't say for certain. I opened the tower's door of eyes with two lines of the Yoal verse. Faramond was behind me when I did that, then everything went black. When I woke up, the tower was gone.'

'On the way up, how did you get past the gargoyle sentinels?'

'I traced the spell for iffryt at each of them, and they left us alone. I reasoned that an iffryt couldn't attack a fellow iffryt.'

'What about the girl who was with you?'

'Girl?' He touched his forehead. 'Ohhh, my head hurts!'

'Faramond said there was one,' Yolantha snapped.

'I don't remember a girl.'

'Now just you see here!' shouted Faramond.

'Silence!' barked Yolantha. 'What about the giant cat?'

'The one that ate the chitterlings? I told Faramond about it, but he didn't believe me.'

'Faramond said it carried you two all the way to the tower,' Yolantha challenged.

'We travelled to it in the sand cart. Most of the way. Then the rear axle broke and we pushed it over a cliff.'

'Probably due to your master's weight,' said Yolantha.

'Lies, all lies!' wailed Faramond.

'Did anything happen to the glass phial containing Elvar?'

'It was gone when I woke up.'

Yolantha turned to Faramond. 'I see everything so clearly now. Winston did all the work, then you struck him from behind! You then protected yourself within the tower with the phial and my iffryt, Elvar.'

'He lies. I never went within a mile of the tower,' Faramond blurted before he caught himself.

'So now you change your story?' asked Yolantha. 'Faramond, put the key's chain around your neck.'

Realising that his only hope was not to annoy Yolantha any further, Faramond did as he was told.

'*Accipatore*,' Yolantha said from the flames, while a hand trailing sparks traced a spell in the air.

The chain immediately tightened. Faramond gasped, trying to remove it, but it became trapped by his bulging wattle.

'Every day the chain will tighten a little more, because a link will disappear,' Yolantha continued. 'In twenty days, the chain will start to cut off your breath. In thirty days, you will be dead, unless I remove it. Be at Highport before thirty days are past, and . . . and what are these drops falling on my head?'

'We're, ah, roasting a goat for the journey home,' said Faramond.

'You summoned me into a cooking fire, you filthy pig?'

'Wood is scarce, we could only build one fire.'

'I think I like Winston's version of the story better,' said Yolantha. 'He cleared the way up the mountain to the door, he opened the door, then you struck him over the head and took the Imperium Key for yourself. Wait a moment! The phial and my iffryt should have protected you within the tower, but they couldn't have.

Gragerian of Merk tried that seven centuries ago and he died.'

'I was leading the way, right up the mountain,' insisted Faramond.

'You've never led the way, except to the dining table. Who destroyed the tower?' Yolantha demanded.

Faramond was trying to do what he did best – dodge liability. 'Destroyed is such a strong word.' Faramond wrung his hands. 'Vanished is more—'

'*Who?*'

'Winston!' Faramond said.

'What do you say to that, Winston?' demanded Yolantha.

'It was gone when I awoke, Ladyship.'

'Faramond, you idiot!' shouted Yolantha. 'The tower was not just an iffryt dressed up as a pile of stones – it was a portal to another world. Now it's gone. Do you know what else is gone? Every iffryt in our own world! All of them! I sent you there to recover the Imperium Key, not to cripple our greatest source of magic!'

'We can always conjure more.'

'Who taught you magical arts?' demanded Yolantha. 'Nobody has been able to conjure a new iffryt since the Imperium Key was lost inside the tower. The tower was the *only* gateway between our world and the iffryt world.'

'But all the iffryts that are already in our world—'

'The tower was more than a portal, it was a valve, preventing them from escaping home. Once the valve was opened, the iffryts flew back in a few heartbeats.'

'From the furthest corners of the world? Impossible.'

'You call yourself a wizard yet you don't know the theory of iffryts? They can be summoned over vast distances in less time than it takes you to belch. Once summoned and given form, they are bound to this material world, and are no faster than a horse or bird. When you destroyed the tower, they cast off their material bodies, streaked back to the portal, then sealed it shut.'

'Surely we can just open another portal?'

'Not without an iffryt! Be at Highport when I arrive there.'

'When will you arrive, Ladyship?'

'Before the chain strangles you, but not long before.'

An arm of flames reached out and seized Faramond's robes, setting them alight. As he rolled about on the ground, screaming and tearing his clothes off, the face vanished from the flames.

'I estimate that we will have to walk twelve miles tomorrow, Master,' said Winston, breaking the silence that followed as Faramond put his burnt robes back on.

'Twelve miles?' Faramond exclaimed. 'Why?'

'To rendezvous with Lady Yolantha before you are strangled by the chain.'

In frustration, Faramond spread his hands. 'I meant why can't your iffryt carry us?'

'There are no more iffryts in our world, Master.'

'Idiot boy, letting them all escape.'

A distant howl echoed amid the mountains.

Faramond spun around. 'What was that?'

'The landlord of the wayfarer's tavern just outside Kalderial said there are wolves in these mountains,' said Winston. 'Also bears, brigands, snow panthers and man-eating packs of mountain boars.'

'You can't leave me alone here.'

'I wasn't going to, Master.'

'But I can only manage five miles in a day.'

'Then we shall take two months to reach Highport. Yolantha will be waiting there in less than thirty days, and you will be strangled before—'

'All right, all right, I will have to manage twelve miles a day. You lied to the High Sorceress, you wretched boy.'

'But Master, you taught me to always do as you're doing, and you were lying to her.'

'Do as I say, boy, not as I do!'

It turned out that Faramond could indeed walk twelve miles in a day. He wasn't happy about it, though. Winston took care to walk about ninety paces ahead of him, so that he could talk to Elvar.

I could tear the old fraud's head off and recover the key, said Elvar in Winston's mind.

'Apparently, the Imperium Key protects the wearer,' replied Winston. 'He can't be killed until Yolantha herself removes the enchanted chain from his neck.'

He's invulnerable? Then what about the chain strangling him after thirty days?

'At a guess, I would say Yolantha was bluffing.'

I could try slashing him to pieces and settle the question.

'Perhaps not,' replied Winston, after a slight but significant hesitation.

We could blame the wolves.

'No!' said Winston firmly. 'Are you sure you can't transform into a giant cat again and carry us to Highport?'

I am bound by different rules of enchantment, now that I share your body. Besides, that would show Faramond – and thus Yolantha – that there is still one iffryt left in the world. She would never stop hunting me, because I could be used to open the portal again.

'Elvar, how much do you know about the Imperium Key's powers?'

They are very potent and highly dangerous.

'Can Faramond use them?'

Yes, but he does not seem to be aware of what he can do, or we would be in a lot of trouble. So would Yolantha.

That is probably because he is such a poor scholar, from what I have seen of him.

'What about when she removes it from him? Will she have those powers?'

I am afraid so.

'What will she do?'

Remember how you learned to draw energies from Faramond and use them to do castings?

'Aye.'

With the Imperium Key, Yolantha can chain dozens, or even hundreds of wizards together, and use their combined powers.

'Maybe I should leave the wizarding profession while it's still safe.'

Winston, Winston, do not be a fool. That is like saying the leak is not at your end of the ship, so you are safe.

Faramond's feet were blistered and bleeding at the end of the first day, and after bolting down more than his ration of the cold roasted goat meat, he fell asleep at once. This gave Winston plenty of time to spear fish and hunt birds for himself. After another ten days it was obvious that Faramond was losing weight due to the exercise. It was also due to having his diet restricted, because each night he had barely enough energy to eat whatever was put aside for him before falling asleep.

'Stupid place to have a road,' he muttered as he re-bandaged his feet on the eleventh morning. 'We've seen nobody else for days. Whoever heard of a road that nobody uses?'

'It was once used by carts from the tin and silver mines in the western Harst Mountains,' said Winston. 'Then a road was built through Watershed Pass, and the journey from the mines was reduced by a third. Only hunters and trappers travel the eastern part of the road now.'

'How do you know all that?'

'I talk to people like traders, merchants, carters, camel drivers and tinsmiths, Master.'

'But they're not wizards!'

'They still know useful things.'

'Only wizards know anything useful.'

Evidently not, mused Winston.

Faramond picked a charred stick out of the campfire, stood up unsteadily and wrote *Faramond was here* on a milestone that declared **HIGHPORT 100**.

'Boy, can you walk thirty-three miles a day for the next three days?' he asked.

'Easily, Master. But why?'

'Because I want to promise myself that in three days, I can be lying on a soft bed in a warm room with my feet up, being tended by a healer with soft, gentle hands while a serving maid feeds me roast pork carved fresh from the spit.'

Faramond managed to keep up with Winston for the first five hours, but by noon the youth was again walking alone. Every so often Faramond would scream with pain and hurry along a bit faster as the shackle spell burned his feet. Much to Winston's surprise, Faramond managed to keep walking all day, and they made camp at the sixty-six milestone.

Winston was noticing some subtle changes to his own body. Apprentices had to shave, because by tradition only wizards had beards. Winston had never seen the guidelines for provisional wizards who weren't yet inducted into the Countercasts' Guild, so he had continued shaving. Now his beard had stopped growing. In fact, it had not produced any stubble for eleven days. Eleven days ago, Elvar had merged with him. Had she stopped him getting any older, or had she made him somewhat less masculine? This was such a sensitive subject that Winston couldn't even discuss it with her.

He was also wondering about Yolantha. She clearly believed that Winston had done most of the work to retrieve the Imperium Key. She was probably impressed. How does she know so much? he wondered. Wizards three times her age weren't as skilled as her. Had she also merged with an iffryt?

The consequences were not entirely clear to him. If that were true, her iffryt had fled the world of humans with all the other iffryts when the portal closed. If an iffryt had preserved Yolantha against the slow onslaught of time, she would now be getting older again. It was no wonder she was so angry when she appeared in the flames of their campfire.

Faramond was so pleased to reach the thirty-three milestone that he put his arms around it and kissed it. Winston fished in the river for dinner, set up camp, gathered firewood, roasted the fish he'd caught, and set up a blanket as a tent for Faramond. The sun was already behind the western peaks as Faramond finished re-bandaging his feet, and he was so famished that he ate his fish without removing the scales, bones, fins or head.

'Any more?' he asked.

'I'll see if I can hunt out a rabbit,' said Winston.

'But it's almost dark.'

'Rabbits come out to feed after dark. The eagles don't hunt at night.'

'You said snow panthers do.'

Winston allowed himself a mental grin. 'They prefer humans.'

'That's not funny! Oi, I'll have to unbandage my feet if you go hunting.'

'So you don't want the rabbit, Master?'

'Oh, get on your way, curse you,' muttered Faramond as he set about unbandaging his feet.

Once clear of the campsite and out of earshot, Elvar was free to speak with Winston.

About tomorrow, she said.

'You mean the meeting with Yolantha?'

Yes. We are in danger.

'Surely no more in danger than Faramond, and probably less,' said Winston.

There is another type of danger, warned Elvar. *I have been thinking about it as we travelled. Remember, I am the only iffryt left in your world. That means someone with the right skills could use me to open another portal to my world, and to summon more of my kind and enslave them again.*

'Someone like Yolantha? Yes, we've already discussed this.'

It will not be a good idea for her to find out about our special arrangement. I wonder if Faramond suspects anything.

'He's told her one lie too many. She'd never believe him.'

But if she were grasping at straws, she might try some simple tests on you.

Winston froze. 'Tests?'

Locking you in a cage and checking whether your fingernails, toenails, beard and hair are growing.

'They're not.'

That is because my presence slows your ageing rate right down to mine, and I age at least fifty times more slowly than a human. Eventually, she will notice, and I am the only chance that the wizards have of restoring magic powered from the iffryt world. Unless you want to spend an eternity as a tower, holding a portal open between two worlds, be on your guard and be ready to flee at all times.

'Gah! Thanks for the warning. Just one more matter?'

Speak, while we are still alone.

'There's a rabbit over there, and within bowshot.'

Yolantha's face appeared in the campfire's flames when Winston walked out of the darkness carrying the rabbit. Faramond was sitting out of reach of her fiery arms.

'Yolantha is already in Highport,' Faramond announced as Winston dropped the rabbit and bowed before her.

'You will set off at first light tomorrow,' said the sorceress. 'Walk faster than your usual pace, and you can be in Highport by mid-afternoon.'

'But my feet . . .' began Faramond.

'Would you like me to turn them into hooves?' asked Yolantha.

Faramond quickly tucked his feet beneath his robe.

'Then endure the pain and keep up with Winston. We shall spend tomorrow night in Highport, then leave for Kalderial.'

'Only one night?' said Faramond in dismay. 'But why must we go with you?'

'Because I'm the head of the order!' shouted Yolantha.

Rather than say any more, the sorceress traced a burning spell in the air with a fiery finger, hissed '*Vortextrias*!' and pointed at Faramond. Immediately a whirlwind of sparks and flames sprang up within the fire, then rushed across to engulf Faramond. Shrieking, he tore off his burning robe and trail cloak, but the burning vortex remained focused on him. It wasn't until he ran naked and screaming to the river and plunged in that Yolantha's casting was extinguished.

That stopped the whirlwind fire from hurting him. Yolantha knew it would do that, said Elvar within Winston's head. *She just wanted to give him a really bad fright.*

'I'm fairly sure she managed that,' whispered Winston.

Naked, smeared with mud and soot, but

otherwise unharmed, Faramond sat on the milestone. The rabbit roasted on a spit while Winston sewed a blanket into an approximation of a smock. The wizard was shivering, but too frightened to approach the fire.

Now, there's a sight, said Elvar.

Winston nodded but said nothing. He handed the completed smock to Faramond, then offered him the roasted rabbit.

'I've lost my appetite,' Faramond mumbled.

'Cheer up, Master. I'll use the rabbit skin to cushion your feet for tomorrow's trek.'

'Which will take us to Yolantha, in person. Why is my life so wretched? I'm not a bad person.'

Just greedy, cruel, bad-tempered, lazy, stupid and arrogant, said Elvar.

They reached the farms and pastures surrounding Highport late in the morning the following day, and by noon were in a hamlet with a tavern where they could buy pies, cheese and bread. Faramond refused to budge from the taproom, and sat with his bare feet on a table while Winston went out into the tiny market and bought clothes to replace the modified blanket that he'd made for Faramond. He also bought a leather tunic for himself, but hid it in his pack.

Something bad is going to happen at Kalderial, Elvar's voice said as he wandered among the stalls.

'Story of my life,' replied Winston.

Something particularly bad. Yolantha worries me.

'Why? It's Faramond who's on the sharp end of her suspicions.'

She is planning something. I have been with her for ten years and I know her moods. She acts as if she is managing some great endeavour.

'Or she's frightened because she noticed she's getting old again now that her iffryt is gone. Perhaps she's just found her first grey hair or wrinkle.'

True. Immortality can be very addictive.

'Is there any way for Yolantha to un-merge us?'

No need. She only has to catch us while I am in iffryt form and she can use the Imperium Key and myself to open a new portal to my world.

'And I would be trapped as well?'

Definitely. Do you fancy living millennia as a tower?

'It's a depressing prospect,' Winston said, 'and I have loftier ambitions.'

I hope you are not planning a career as a fairground jester, said Elvar.

The sun was among the mountain peaks in the west when they reached Highport. They passed a waterfall that plunged fifteen hundred feet over a cliff, then became a placid river that meandered over the wide, flat plain that extended two hundred miles to the sea. Highport was not the highest river port in the world, but it had been the first to use the name, so most people assumed that there was none higher.

Two militiamen met them at the city gates, and to Faramond's delight they had a donkey cart waiting for him. Yolantha had taken over the entire upper floor of the Waterfall's Rest tavern.

'Silly name,' said Faramond, stepping down from the cart. 'Waterfalls never rest.'

Yolantha was waiting at the door. She was dressed in fine and expensive clothes, but they were practical and well-suited to travel. What she was wearing would have been perfect had she been a general or prince setting off to battle at the head of an army. Her cloak was thick and had a rain hood, and she wore leather trousers and knee boots. Whatever else she was wearing was obscured by chainmail, and this included fine chainmail gloves. Her sword and scabbard had no gemstones or precious metals decorating them. That suggested that the sword was for killing people, and Winston reminded himself that she might have many lifetimes' worth of fencing experience behind her sword arm.

'You're late,' she said, glaring at Faramond.

'Apologies, Ladyship, we did our best,' he fawned, bowing low with a hand pressed against his ample belly.

'Your best included two hours in a hamlet's tavern, according to the birds that see all.'

'Oh, er, yes, but I – we – wanted to clean up and look our best for you.'

Yolantha traced a spell and directed it at Faramond. The missing links in the chain holding the Imperium Key materialised at once, and Faramond wasn't slow to remove it from his neck. He held it out to her. She snatched it from him without touching his hand. Now facing Winston, she traced a spell then clapped. Immediately the smell of baking bread and roasting meat vanished from his nostrils. She did the same for Faramond, who gave a yelp, then rubbed at his feet.

'They can't be burning,' said Winston. 'I'm only ten feet away.'

'That was the shackle spell breaking,' said Yolantha. 'They would have only tingled for a moment.'

'But you didn't heal them as well.'

'Would you like the shackle spell back, Faramond?'

'No, no, I've grown skilled with healing spells and bandages.'

'Well, seeing you two have already cleaned up and eaten, there is no need for you to stay in the tavern overnight,' declared Yolantha. 'I have a barge hired and waiting at the docks. The road to Kalderial is a hundred and twenty miles down the river, and with the current behind us we can get there in less than two days.'

'There's two more days of walking after that,' Faramond pointed out.

'I can arrange a donkey for you,' Yolantha said.

Faramond's eyebrows shot up. 'That would be acceptable.'

'Do you think you can carry a donkey?'

'Ah, perhaps not, but . . .'

'But?'

Faramond cleared his throat nervously, the rumblings from his stomach momentarily outweighing his fear of Yolantha.

'But Ladyship, I only managed to make that terrible journey on time by promising myself the prospect of a properly cooked dinner in a tavern, and at least one night in a nice comfortable bed.'

'Dinner? Bed?' she said. 'I'll give you dinner and a bed.'

She traced two spells, then, reaching out with both hands, crushed them in her fingers and flung two clouds of sparkles at Faramond. After a moment every vegetable, roast chicken, pie and sausage in the inn's kitchen came rushing out on little legs. Faramond screamed, turned and fled down the street, pursued by the food he had desired so much. Shortly after, a bed burst through an upstairs window, landed in the street, then went galloping after the wizard.

Yolantha leaned against the doorframe of the

inn, then slowly sank to the steps. 'That required a lot of effort, but it was worth it,' she said to Winston.

'What will happen when they catch him, Ladyship?'

'Once he is exhausted and is forced to stop, he will realise that they cannot get closer to him than a yard or so. If he chases them, they will run away. Eventually he will realise that if he wants food that will stand still and cooperate, he will have to get aboard the barge.'

The barge carried eight horses, six pack donkeys, Yolantha's six mercenaries, Yolantha, Faramond and Winston. They disembarked at Earthshift Landing. This was where an earthquake had changed the course of the Harst River long ago, depriving Kalderial of its water supply and link to the ocean. This was also where Yolantha had what looked like a small city of tents waiting. There were five hundred more mercenaries, six huge ox carts, three dozen oxen, and more servants and pack donkeys than Winston could count. There were also three hundred unemployed wizards. Yolantha told Faramond and Winston to join the other wizards, but Winston slipped away as soon as it was evening.

'I'll not be missed for days in that crowd,' he said as he hid amid roadside trees, changing into the leather tunic of a journeyman metalsmith.

Do you have any metalsmith skills, in case someone asks? Elvar asked in his head.

'I'll say I'm an apprentice travelling to my new master. It's time for us to vanish from the world of wizards. My plan is to walk through the night and reach Kalderial sometime tomorrow. There I can retrieve my books from Griffid's hoard, and we can go on to Haldan.'

Is there anything special about Haldan?

'Yes. They have a mundane academy there.'

An academy that does not teach any magic at all?

'Aye, so Yolantha won't bother with it. The Royal Academy of Cold Sciences will take anyone who can pass their entrance exams, and produces enough money. Even better, one is admitted at the year equal to one's score in the entrance exam. I'm pretty good with herbalist theory and practice, and I've managed to read about anatomy and suchlike.'

There has to be a catch.

'There is. One pays for a five-year certificate, even if one only needs to study for the last two years. I can meet the fee if I don't bother eating and don't mind sleeping under bridges.'

Why turn your back on wizardry? You have a natural talent for it.

'Yolantha will be looking for someone who dresses like a wizard and uses magic to pay for rent and food. As a physician of the cold sciences, I will be invisible to her.'

I look forward to a life of lancing boils, splinting broken limbs and prescribing dried herbs and powdered insects for fevers, Elvar joked.

'Would you prefer to be a tower enclosing a portal to your world?'

A good point, Elvar conceded.

'Then you and I are about to become an academy student.'

Why are we walking? We're clear of Yolantha's encampment now, so you can morph me back into my true form and we can fly to Kalderial.

'No! Bad idea.'

Why?

'Yolantha is sure to have her watchbirds scattered around, spying for her. One or two are probably spying on us this minute, but all they see is a journeyman's apprentice.'

True.

'Then there's the morphings. When you morphed into my form at the base of Blackstone Mountain, it was days before I recovered from the fatigue. Even now I don't feel at my best.'

I noticed.

'I have been thinking about the way magic has changed since the tower vanished. There are no more energies flowing from a portal to your world. It's part of the cost of liberating your people, or whatever it is you call them. The energies for all morphings have to come from this world.'

From eating food?

'Yes.'

That is a very slow and inefficient way to hoard energies. Winston, you have an annoying way of being right about things I wish you were wrong about.

'Sorry. Just now we really do have to walk to Kalderial, but it's only thirty miles. Yolantha's watchbirds will roost during the night, even though the moon is up, so if we continue walking, they will lose us. Yolantha will assume I wanted to go home to Loseros and took the left branch in the road, instead of going right to Kalderial.'

I am learning a lot from you, Winston.

'All of it rat cunning, I fear.'

What is wrong with that? Just about everything is bigger and stronger than a rat, yet there are still plenty of rats.

Chapter Seven

Griffid stretched languidly beneath a towering orchestra tree, a magical creation that had been the centrepiece of a very rich aristocrat's garden in a bygone era. Its funnel fronds played tunes on the wind like a living organ, while tendril-thin vines vibrated like the strings of a harp. Brightly-coloured birds chirped in the branches above his head, like a choir singing along with the tree.

The general feeling of contentment vanished when he felt a sting. He opened his eyes and slowly raised his head. Before Griffid was a young warrior on a battle horse. His armour was moderately well-fashioned, although the mailshirt was too large. The breastplate verged on being antique, which was quite a surprise for the dragon. Another surprise was the Riverhead crest painted on it, because Riverhead had been abandoned almost as long ago as Kalderial. A broken lance was in the hands of whoever it was. The pointy end had broken off and was sticking in Griffid.

In spite of what trashy ballads say, knights cannot kill dragons, said Griffid in Larissa's mind.

She ignored the deep, echoing voice. There were three more lances leaning against a nearby tree, and she was obviously at least moderately strong, because breaking a lance required a lot of muscle power. She discarded the broken lance and rode back for another, then urged the horse into a charge.

The horse was the veteran of dozens of tournaments and even a couple of minor wars, so it was experienced where combat was concerned. Nevertheless, his rider was attacking something bigger than the stables where it normally lived. More to the point, it had woken up and was staring at him. The horse did what any sensible and battle-hardened horse would do under the circumstances. It stopped, reared, and bucked its rider off. It then trotted off a short distance and began to graze, to give the dragon and human a chance to sort out their differences by negotiation.

The girl drew her sword and ran at Griffid, shouting about how she was doing it for the honour of the House of Riverhead. Griffid lashed out with his long tail, smashing her through the air and against a tree. Here she lay stunned for some moments before getting up and retrieving her sword.

This time she staggered toward the dragon, rather than charged. Griffid thought about turning her into charcoal floating on a puddle of molten iron, but then decided that he wanted to hear her story, whatever it was. Again, he lashed at her with his tail, but this time he wrapped the end around her, pinning her arms and lifting her high off the ground. She could do no more than writhe and squeal with rage.

What is all this about? asked the dragon, his voice like a thunderclap within her head.

'Let me go!' she yelled.

I asked a question. I want an answer or there will be consequences.

'Fight honourably.'

You lanced me while I slept, how honourable was that?

'Let me go.'

Ah, you want consequences.

Griffid uncoiled his tail in an instant. He had been holding her ten feet above the ground, however, so when she hit what had once been a garden plaza's flagstones, it was with an impressive impact. She didn't move again. Griffid got to his feet, stretched, took a deep breath, then inclined his head back and blew a streamer of flame high into the air. He peered down at the girl, who had managed to retrieve her sword in a triumph of bravery over common sense. Griffid took an even deeper breath, opened his jaws and looked down at her.

'Oi, Griffid, it's all right, she's one of ours.'

Griffid looked up and saw a youth approaching along the overgrown path that might once have been a road.

Winston? the dragon spoke in his mind. *Where are your robes?*

'Change of career. I see you have a piece of timber stuck in your backside.'

Don't ask.

'Can I offer my services as a healer?'

Healer?

'Unless that lance sticking in you is some sort of fashion declaration.'

Oh, that. Please go ahead.

This feat of healing turned out to be easier said than done. Winston had to catch Larissa's horse, tie one end of a rope to the saddle horn and the other end to the broken piece of lance, then tempt the horse forward with a carrot from his pack. Griffid could have eventually extracted the lance tip with his teeth, but Winston thought it important to put on a display of goodwill. He now turned his attention to the girl, who had climbed to her knees, still holding her sword.

'I'll never surrender!' she shouted, even though she had quite clearly been defeated.

As far as she was concerned, if Winston had helped the dragon, he was the enemy as well.

Given the choice of a spear or a sword, which does the battle-wise warrior choose? Winston was no warrior, but having grown up in the grubby and dangerous alleyways of Loseros, he'd learned that six feet of pole beats a knife any time. It can also beat a sword, unless whoever wields the sword knows what to do when confronted with two yards of a wayfarer's hardwood staff. Larissa's fencing master had taught her that the sword was the prince of weapons. He had not taught her that the tip of a spear or quarterstaff moves considerably faster than the tip of a sword, and has twice the reach.

Chroniclers are paid to write flattering histories by rich nobles, and if ten enemy nobles lie dead after a battle, the chronicler is going to give the credit to the rich noble rather than the peasants who killed those nobles with long, sharp sticks shoved through gaps in their armour. A lot of Larissa's martial arts theory had been learned from chronicles, which meant that it was about as useful to her as a bottle of rosewater would have been to Winston's younger sister and her terrier.

Slowly and shakily, Larissa got to her feet and lunged at Winston. He swayed back then thrust out with the blunt tip of his staff, striking Larissa's helmet just above the eye slit. He dodged to the right and forward as she staggered backwards, thrusting his staff into the soil behind her. She tripped and fell flat on her back. Winston stood on the blade of her sword.

What school of fencing is that? asked Griffid in their minds.

'The Staying Alive Academy,' said Winston as

he removed Larissa's three daggers.

You know her?

'We've met.'

Larissa's nose was bleeding, and her face was red from exertion, or mortification, or both. When she sat up, Winston pointed at Griffid with one of her daggers.

'This is a dragon – *dracondaris nobillatem ignitare*, if you want to get technical,' he said.

Nobilaten, corrected Griffid.

'Note his size. He's at least two hundred times your weight, probably more. Now watch carefully.'

Winston walked over to Griffid and jabbed at one of his scales with the dagger. He might as well have jabbed a steel plate.

'You managed to get your lance tip between his scales because you caught him asleep. When awake he can reduce you to a very small pile of charcoal or a very large red smear. Yes, I know you're thinking that your armour will protect you. Griffid, show the lady what dragons do to armour. Oh, and burn my old robe while you're about it.'

Winston removed his wizard's robe from his

pack, draped it over the trunk of a fallen tree, and placed Larissa's helmet on top of it. He walked well clear. Griffid drew breath, then poured out a stream of fire over the target.

'You will note that the tree and everything behind it for a hundred yards or so has been annihilated, the flagstones of the old garden plaza are glowing red, my robe is ash, and your helmet is a small pool of iron.'

Larissa sat wide-eyed with astonishment. When chroniclers described dragons, they merely wrote that they breathed fire and had wings. None of them had ever seen a real dragon breathing fire, and quite probably, none of them had seen a real dragon, either. Larissa had thought dragon fire was like the flames that burned wood beneath the cauldron in the family mansion's kitchen. Now she realised that a dragon's flames could melt the cauldron.

'I am now going to take your armour off and check your injuries,' said Winston.

'What? Never, you filthy swine.'

'It's all right, the dragon can be your chaperone.'

'But—'

'And my mother is the herbalist, Molly Spellwyn.'

The name commanded instant respect. Winston's mother had saved many lives and had been the midwife at the birth of both Larissa and her younger sister.

'Mother Spellwyn?' she said in a more reasonable tone. 'Oh. I suppose that's all right, then.'

As Winston examined Larissa, he counted eleven strains, two sprains, five contusions, a broken rib, a wrenched left shoulder and many splotches of reddish bruising. There were sure to be more beneath her undergarments, but she was reluctant to remove those.

'I'm impressed,' said Winston with genuine admiration. 'Anyone else would be screaming with pain, including me.'

'Was that meant to be a compliment?' asked Larissa, her voice sullen.

'I was pointing out that you have been badly hurt, mainly by being smashed about by a dragon, then dropped from a great height onto stone paving. I'm surprised you're even alive.'

'My armour protected me.'

'Only the plate armour. Chainmail is close to useless.'

'Then why do knights wear it?'

'It's only good for staving off the nicks you might otherwise have sustained. Now don't go hitting the dragon while I load your weapons and armour onto the horse. Oi, Griffid, I need to take the box of books that I've hidden in your hoard.'

Do so. I am not much of a reader.

'And what about a few shillings for pulling the lance out?'

No! I spared the girl's life at your request. That is your reward.

With Larissa on the horse, along with her armour, weapons and Winston's box of books, they made their way to the hideaway that Winston had built for when he wanted to hide from Faramond. He left Larissa there to rest while he gathered firewood.

Do you like the girl? asked Elvar once they were alone.

'No.'

Then why rescue her?

'It was the decent thing to do.'

You are decent, but not as decent as that. Winston, she has the survival skills of a moth in love with a candle flame. Why bother?

'If you must know, when I was little, I dreamed about rescuing a princess from a dragon, being offered her hand in marriage by the king, and living happily ever after in a palace. Well, I've lived in a ruined palace, and that leaves a maiden to be rescued from a dragon.'

You are joking! exclaimed Elvar, who then laughed so much within Winston's mind that he had the beginnings of a headache by the time she stopped. *That is the silliest thing I have ever heard.*

Winston felt his face reddening. 'You didn't get out much over the past three thousand years, did you? Humans do silly things for sillier reasons. Now I've rescued a maiden from a dragon, so everything on my list is ticked off. More or less.'

But she is not a princess.

'Near enough! She's young, female, from the nobility, and I rescued her.'

She was useless as a warrior. Even you were able to beat her.

'Don't judge her too hastily, Elvar. She survived alone in these ruins for all the time that

Faramond and I were away, so she must be tough and resourceful. And don't forget, she was in a lot of pain and badly injured when I fought her. If she'd been at her best, the fight may well have gone against me.'

Two hours later Winston was roasting a hare over a small fire. Larissa had thrown up when he'd skinned and gutted the animal in front of her. But now that it resembled something that the family cook might have served for dinner, she had convinced herself that it might be safe to eat.

'Time to talk,' said Winston.

Reluctantly, she looked up. 'I'm Larissa.'

'I know that.'

'How?' she asked, almost instantly regretting her query.

'Mother Spellwyn's shop on rent day. I was the boy chopping up oyster hearts for her special restorative tonic. You were riding a donkey, wearing parchment armour and holding a curtain rod for a lance. You hit me with the curtain rod for laughing at you. And my name's Winston.'

This was not a memory that Larissa was

interested in being reminded of.

'I've nothing else to say,' she muttered.

Winston leant forward in earnest. 'Then *I'll* talk. Do you know how many documented cases there are of fully armoured knights going against a dragon? Probably not. It's three hundred and eighty-one. Do you know how many knights got roasted?'

'I suppose you do.'

'Yes. It's three hundred and eighty-one.'

'My cause is noble.'

'Ladyship, why don't knights charge at enemy castles with lances?'

Larissa hesitated. This was sure to be a trick question, but she couldn't see the trick.

'Castle walls are too strong?' she ventured.

'Correct, and so are dragons. Now why attack a dragon when the chances of winning are absolutely zero?'

'I've already told you; my cause is noble.'

'And futile. Leave Griffid alone. He's harmless unless you're a wild pig, escaped donkey or stray sheep.' Winston thought for a moment. 'Or a rotund wizard with an attitude problem.'

Larissa waved away his obvious attempt at

humour. 'My father's ill. The physician said that dragon brain would cure him.'

Winston took a few seconds to concentrate on not laughing. Elvar laughing hysterically in his mind didn't help.

'Dragon brain?' he said eventually. 'That's a herb.'

'What?'

'You didn't know?'

'It can't be.'

'I gathered, sorted, chopped, dried, powdered and mixed herbs from my third birthday until I was twelve years and eleven months old. Trust me, I know dragon brain. The leaves are dark green and crinkly like walnuts or real brains.'

Larissa didn't reply. *Embarrassment*, said Elvar within his head.

'Don't tell me. The physician told you that dragon brain is to be found in the ruins of Kalderial, so you came here looking for a dragon. If you'd told me what you wanted instead of sneering at me for being a peasant, I would've told you where to find it.'

By now, Larissa's sense of pride had dropped somewhere below zero on a scale of one to ten.

She slumped. 'I've spent months looking for a dragon in these ruins when I should have been looking for a plant,' she muttered, still keeping her emotions in check although she wasn't far off tears.

'Actually, thirty-eight days,' said Winston, who could be annoying when it came to facts.

'My father may be dead because of my stupidity.'

Even without her armour Larissa was still an impressively strong girl – easily stronger than Winston and probably in the same class as his sisters. Winston was not used to seeing anyone humiliated who was not Faramond. For some reason that probably owed more to his sense of chivalry than charity, he decided to help.

'I'll go collect some dragon brain for you before sunset,' he said. 'Best you don't travel for a few days after that battering.'

'But I must! My father lies sick and is close to death.'

'Then I'll take the dragon brain to him.'

'When?'

'Tomorrow.'

Alone in a patch of dragon brain, Winston bickered with Elvar while he harvested the leaves.

Why are we helping someone stupid enough to attack a dragon with a lance? said Elvar.

'Because she's stupid yet honourable, and I'm sometimes stupid and usually honourable. She's trying to fight her way out of her circumstances.'

Ah! She reminds you of yourself?

'Yes, and what's wrong with that? When she isn't injured, she can probably hold her own against any foot soldier. Most of my martial experience has been in persuading dinner to come quietly.'

I can fight foot soldiers by the score. We iffryts are good at fighting.

'I would have to transform myself into you first, and that will leave both of us too drained and tired to fight. Besides, as soon as an iffryt is spotted anywhere and word gets back to Yolantha, she'll have every wizard in the known world looking for you – and me. Faramond will be one of them. How long can we hide from that sort of attention?'

You may be right.

'It happens.'

So how do we get the dragon brain to Warrior Girl's father?

'Loseros is only thirty miles away. I'll sleep here tonight, and walk there tomorrow. I should arrive in the evening. I'll hand over the dragon brain. I can sleep on Mother's floor . . . on second thought, no, she'll charge me rent. I'll start back and sleep in one of Farmer Prescar's haystacks, then walk back. Two days, Larissa should have recovered by then.'

You could borrow her horse.

'No, I couldn't! Any peasant – that's me – caught riding a horse belonging to a noble – that's her – will be accused of having stolen it and be arrested, charged, convicted and hanged the same day. My plan is to walk to Loseros, give the Lord of the Riversend Lancers his dose of dragon brain, wait for him to write a nice scroll explaining to Larissa that he feels a lot better, and return – on foot.'

You are in love.

'No I'm not.'

People in love do stupid things, and this is absolutely stupid.

'That's all very wise and profound, coming from someone who has spent millennia in a bottle.'

Three thousand years watching you humans make fools of yourselves.

The sun was rising when Winston and Elvar set off for Loseros. They walked without a break, bickering all the way about why Winston was going to so much trouble over someone he had spent his entire childhood disliking. Sometime after sunset they reached a large house near the middle of the fishing port.

Are you sure this is the place? asked Elvar. *These houses all look the same to me.*

'Er, no. I remember Larissa's family having a house with a slate roof and glass in every window, and it was surrounded by a high wall. Arry the Cat said he burgled the place once. He said there's a garden behind the wall with tame fish in a pond. There are guard dogs, too. Big, savage beasts.'

All the houses look like that, and I can hear dogs barking behind most of the walls. You're only doing this for Larissa, aren't you?

'I'm doing this because . . . because I'm doing this.'

You like her.

'Rubbish.'

Don't lie.

'I'm peasant class, she's a merchant's daughter, and her family is upper merchant class. Upper merchant class with a father with enough money to buy a title and become lower upper class.'

You hardly know her.

'I've known her for ten years. Her father owns my mother's house. When his scribe called around to collect the rent, Larissa pretended to be his guard and sneer at me.'

Ah, so you hate her. This is a way of proving your superiority.

'I don't hate her, but . . . it would be nice to feel just a little bit superior.'

Now that I can understand. When the old man is cured, will you gloat?

'No.'

What? Why not?

'Because I'm doing this for me, not her.'

This is all too confusing. Do what you like, I will just watch.

A squad of the Loseros Town Militia marched around the corner.

'Oi you, boy!' cried the leader, who was feeling rather pleased with himself for finding someone harmless-looking to challenge. 'What's your business here?'

'Medicinal delivery,' replied Winston. 'Can I be about my business? I have a rare herb to deliver to a sick nobleman.'

'Rare herb. Who – wait a moment, aren't you young Winston Spellwyn, the wizard's apprentice?'

'Provisional wizard, now.'

'Already? Oi, you *are* on the way up.'

'Look, er, Corporal . . . Dashwell, isn't it?'

'Aye, that's me.'

'I've got physician's herbs to deliver from Larissa de Green, the daughter of Hugo de Green, Captain of the Riversend Lancers.'

'Heard about that. He paid a packet to be lord of a town with no people in it. The river stopped flowing and now there's no water in it, so—'

'He bought the title, but he lives here. Look, are you going to keep me here chatting until he dies?'

'Well, no. Suppose you're respectable.'

'Know where he lives?'

'Aye, you can't miss the place. Turn right, first north, then left to the public fountain, then third on the right. It's the house with the big sign saying Captain Hugo de Green, with two lanterns burning on either side to make sure people can read it at night.'

Minutes later, Winston was standing outside the house of the de Greens.

Why have a sign with lanterns? asked Elvar. *Do people need captains in an emergency at night?*

'Captains are the very lowest ranks of the aristocracy, but they like people to *know* that they're aristocracy.'

It took quite a lot of ringing the gate's bell to rouse a footman. He explained that Captain Hugo was sick and couldn't be disturbed. Winston informed him that he was a provisional wizard with a cure. He was escorted past the guard dogs and the scribe was woken. Winston explained, again, why he was there.

Access to the upper floor had to be approved by the steward. He checked the dragon brain in Winston's bag against a picture of the herb in a reference book, then escorted him upstairs. Here, Captain Hugo's wife barred the way. Winston showed her the dragon brain and the steward showed her the picture in the book. Finally, he was escorted into the captain's bedchamber. Winston was silently relieved there was no physician to question his presence as well.

The patient was shaken awake by his wife.

'A young wizard is here with the herb that is specific to your illness,' she said.

The steward took Winston by the arm and led him forward.

'Captain Hugo, I have been told that you are in dire need of dragon brain,' was as far as Winston got.

'Young man, I do hope you have not gone to an excess of trouble to visit me with your wonderful herb, but I am afraid I cannot partake of it.'

Something about the man's voice annoyed both Winston and Elvar intensely. It was probably because he sounded like a lord speaking to his serfs.

'May I respectfully ask why not, Lordship?' asked Winston.

'My brave, beloved elder daughter has gone on a quest to find dragon brain for me. I am honour-bound to take the cure from her hand alone.'

'But she sent me.'

'Ah no, I'm afraid I must be cured by Larissa and no other.'

Back outside on the street, and for the first time in his life, Winston found himself in such a rage that the world seemed to be spinning. He had to steady himself against a wall.

Are you anywhere nearly as angry as I am? asked Elvar.

'You couldn't possibly be as angry as me,' Winston replied.

Would you like me to make us both very, very happy?

'Oh? But at what cost? Yolantha's watchbirds—'

I have not sensed their presence since we entered Kalderial.

'What? Yolantha would never give up on me so easily.'

Yes she would. She has three hundred wizards to keep track of and no more than three dozen watchbirds to do it — I counted them. Find one journeyman's apprentice who might be a worthless, fugitive, fourteen-year-old provisional wizard? Difficult. Find him in the ruins of Kalderial? Impossible, even with every watchbird at her disposal. No, you're too hard to track and anyway, you're unimportant.

'Story of my life.'

You're important to me, Winston. Isn't that better?

'Okay, okay.'

Although it was probably not a good idea after walking thirty miles, and before having dinner, Winston traced the spell, spoke the word and transformed into Elvar. With one great beat of her wings, she launched herself into the air, circled the house once, then dived at the part of the roof where she estimated that Captain Hugo lay dying.

A few well-placed slashes of her talons tore away the slates of the roof. She then ripped the bearers out and plunged through the hole, continuing on through the ceiling below. Landing on the captain's bed, Elvar seized the man by the throat.

'Now listen well, dotard, you are going to take your dragon brain or I am going to get angry!' she shouted in his face. 'Is that clear?'

Before he could reply, the door was thrown open and the captain's wife entered. She took one look at Elvar, screamed and fainted. Behind her was the steward. He turned and ran, shouting for the dogs and the town militia. After a moment's thought, Elvar flung the blankets aside, seized the captain's leg and launched herself and the captain at the leadlight windows. She burst through, spread her wings and glided to the lawn. The captain was screaming continually, except when drawing breath for another scream.

Elvar landed beside an ornamental pond. Seizing the captain by the throat with her wing claws, she reached into Winston's bag and stuffed a generous measure of dragon brain into his mouth. She then held his face under the water while a school of astonished goldfish looked on in the light of the ornamental lanterns, held by stone dragons with silly grins.

'Drink and swallow!' Elvar shouted.

The captain did so. She dragged his head out of the water and stuffed yet more dragon brain into his mouth.

'Eat! Drink! Swallow! Try to spit it out, and I'll stuff it back in. That's it, everything in the bag! Eat! Eat! Eat!'

Someone finally fetched the guard dogs. They bounded across the lawn, growling, snarling and barking. After one look at Elvar, both dogs turned and fled, scrambling up and over the fifteen-foot wall, leaving trails of faeces and urine in their wake. Neither was ever seen again.

'Feeling cured?' Elvar growled.

'I was never sick,' the captain gasped, his voice hoarse from screaming, eating dragon brain and swallowing pond water.

'You had better have a convincing explanation, or I shall drop you back into your bed from a thousand feet above your house.'

'Please, try to understand. I pretended to be sick so I could send Larissa on a harmless quest to find dragon brain.'

For a few moments, Elvar fought for control. Fortunately for the captain, she won.

'Did it ever cross your mind that your daughter

is more of a warrior than a scholar? She tried to extract the brains from a real dragon instead of seeking the herb.'

'There's a real dragon in the ruins?' stuttered the captain.

'All fifteen tons of one, yes,' replied Elvar.

'By all the demons of the underworld! Is Larissa all right?'

'Yes, but only by chance. Get up. Call for pen, parchment and sealing wax.'

'What do you mean? What for?'

'You're going to write and seal a scroll telling Larissa that the young man she sent to Loseros found you and gave you the herb that she gathered – and that you're feeling much better. Oh, and she'll need a spare helmet, her other one was damaged by the dragon.'

Chapter Eight

'It does one good to let one's temper off the leash every so often,' said Elvar as she flew back to Kalderial with the rising sun behind her.

I suppose you caused less of a scene than Griffid would have, but not much less, Winston replied within her head.

'Are you still going to tell her that Griffid flew you to Loseros?'

Yes.

'Her father will eventually point out to her that I am a lot smaller than the average dragon.'

Probably, but by then I'll have made up some plausible lies to explain the inexplicable.

Faramond had severe doubts about whatever Yolantha was planning because it involved him being soaked in gravy and beef broth just outside Kalderial's Summer Gate. Next, she traced a spell and cast an enchantment on the wizard, one that he was not familiar with. Finally, she tied a rope around his neck, then led him into the city. Very soon the scent emanating from Faramond woke Griffid from his dreams.

'I wish to pay tribute to you, mighty Griffid, so that I may visit these ruins in search of a powerful, ancient amulet,' she called, as the dragon shuffled onto the path leading to the old royal palace.

I see only a senile wizard, said Griffid.

'This wizard has displeased me greatly, and violated the laws of the Countercasts' Guild of Magic. I have condemned him to death.'

Griffid lowered his head and sniffed at Faramond, brushing at him with the sensitive tendrils growing out of the sides of his mouth.

Delicious. How could I possibly refuse?

Griffid opened his jaws and extended an enormous forked tongue which he wrapped around Faramond, then drew him into his mouth. The dragon should have known that something was wrong, because the wizard was not hysterical with fear. However, as was so often the case with

Griffid, his stomach got the better of him. Gently he closed his mouth over the wizard, savouring the taste. Suddenly, glowing gold tendrils boiled out of Faramond, snaking between the astonished dragon's teeth and binding his jaws shut.

Now Yolantha conjured a casting, flinging a golden rope to entangle Griffid's legs, then sending the other end whirling to wrap around the trunk of an old and massive tree. Flap and leap as he might, Griffid was unable to get into the air. Yolantha collapsed to the path from the strain of conjuring a rope strong enough to bind a dragon, but before Griffid thought to hop forward and trample her into bloody mush, her entourage of wizards came rushing out of hiding, flinging yet more golden ropes to bind his legs together. The golden ropes then flew through the air and wrapped his wings against his body.

You betrayed me! shouted Griffid in Faramond's head. He thrashed maniacally, but the more he struggled, the tighter the ropes became.

'And you ate me!' retorted Faramond. 'Fair's fair.'

You should have warned me!

'She was going to drop me into a barrel of

hungry river crays if I didn't do as she said.'

'Now I do hope you two are going to get along!' said Yolantha, standing with one foot on Griffid's head. 'You are about to go on a short journey aboard six wagons tied together in a line, then a longer journey to Highport on three barges tethered in a row, then a much longer journey on another six wagons through the Harst Mountains to Blackstone Mountain. It will take months.'

'Lady Yolantha, why can't I be released now?' called Faramond.

'Don't you know your dragon anatomy?' asked Yolantha. 'Dragons can't breathe fire unless their jaws are open, otherwise they would burn their own teeth. Griffid's jaws must stay bound.'

Morach, where are you? called Griffid in their minds. *Why didn't you warn me that a whole army was on the way?*

A woman of perhaps thirty, wearing black silk robes and with gleaming white hair that reached below her waist, sauntered up and stood beside Yolantha.

'Lady Yolantha made me an offer I couldn't refuse,' she said.

Morach?

'You know, Griffid, I much prefer living a short, mortal life to immortality as a bird.'

'Three Countercast wizards nearly starved to death breaking that curse, but I have ways of forcing wizards to cooperate,' said Yolantha. 'Remember that, Faramond.'

When Winston and Elvar returned to the deserted city, one fact stood out very clearly: it wasn't deserted. Elvar landed hurriedly in the ruins of a watchtower, from which there was a view of the intruders. There were more than a thousand of them.

'All the men, wizards, oxen and ox carts from Earthshift are here,' said Elvar, after scanning the scene for just a moment. 'The carts are all tied together to make one big, long wagon, and Griffid is on top of them.'

I can see all that too, I'm using the same eyes, said Winston.

'No need for sarcasm.'

The bindings are magical, I recognise the casting. They must've needed a huge amount of magical resources. Only Yolantha could have organised this.

'How is she paying all these people? It would take a king's ransom.'

Or a dragon's hoard. She's probably looting Griffid's as we speak.

'Why does she want a dragon?'

Griffid isn't just any dragon. He's the only dragon that doesn't live on the island of Dracondas. He was expelled for doing something that dragons find offensive; nobody is sure what. Dragons weigh about as much as three forest elephants, and that's fifteen tons. Let me think on this. A strong man could walk upstairs wearing a pack weighing a hundred and fifty pounds. Based on that, two hundred and twenty-four men could carry a dragon up Blackstone Mountain.

'Except the stairs aren't wide enough.'

Perhaps carry was the wrong word, but more on that later. That chain of carts carrying Griffid would be lucky to make four miles a day. That's a hundred days to reach Blackstone Mountain.

'We could easily fly there first.'

And do what?

'Portals are highly unstable when they are being set up. We could disrupt this one.'

Are they undefended as well?

'That may be a problem, unless we get there first and choose our moment carefully.'

Well, for now we should morph back into me and find Larissa. I need to know about what happened here over the past day.

Elvar traced the morphing spell with a claw and spoke the word for human. Her image flickered and blurred, then the mass of red fur made several attempts to become Winston, as if too weak to complete the task. Having finally recovered his true form, Winston passed out.

It was around sunset when Winston woke. He managed to sit up, but not without difficulty.

Winston rubbed his eyes. 'Am I allowed to ask what happened?'

Depletion sickness, replied Elvar.

'From morphing?'

Yes. We have exchanged shapes twice in two days, and both times depleted your life force, not to mention your body fat and muscles. I thought you could last longer, but you were underweight to start with.

'How long does it take to recover? I feel really bad.'

I feel the same. I estimate it will be three months before you can again morph safely.

Winston managed to crawl back to his vantage spot. The soldiers, ox carts and Griffid were all gone. Very slowly and carefully, he crawled his way down the ruins of the tower. He thought about standing up, then decided that it wasn't a good idea. He was less of a target on all fours, and the actual effort of standing was probably beyond him anyway. All of a sudden, he felt the cold steel of a sword blade pressed against the back of his neck.

'Just kill me and get it over with,' said Winston, recognising Larissa's boots. 'Nobody who feels as bad as I do should be alive.'

'That's not playing fair,' said Larissa.

Elvar seethed within Winston, so much so he slumped further to the ground.

'*Pfft!*' Larissa said. Taking Winston by the arm, she heaved, then promptly fell over backwards. Winston followed and landed on top of her.

'Winston!' she shrieked. 'You weigh less than my little sister!'

This might just be because he's very sick! grumbled Elvar.

Larissa had no difficulty at all carrying Winston to where she'd been hiding. He devoured the little meat she had there. She explained that when Yolantha and her small army arrived, she had hidden her horse deeper in the ruins, then returned to watch.

'Did you manage to reach my father?' she asked at last.

'Your father is alive and cured,' Winston said, taking the scroll from his robes and handing it to her.

Larissa broke the seal and read the scroll.

'Yes, yes, this is his writing and seal. The dragon brain worked!'

No, it didn't, said Elvar, wishing that Larissa could hear her.

'But how did you reach Loseros and return in just two days?' asked Larissa.

'I have access to wings,' said Winston.

'What? No, you don't. I see no wings.'

'Really, I do.'

'You're just trying to fool me. You think I'm a silly girl who believes anything she's told.'

'Larissa, you believed that your father was sick just because he told you so!' Winston snapped, finally running out of patience and diplomacy. 'He wasn't sick at all. He was never sick! He was forced to write that letter after a dragon dunked his head in his own ornamental fish pond.'

'Nonsense, his dogs would have rescued him.'

'Did you catch the word dragon? Huge flappy thing, covered in scales, breathes fire, eats people and is willing to consider dogs.'

Larissa thought about his words, then about her father and the way he solved problems by giving people precisely what they asked for, instead of what they actually wanted.

'Why would my father be so cruel?' she cried. 'Why would he play such a heartless joke on me?'

'So you would have to sleep in the open, travel in rain, catch, kill and cook your own meals, bathe in cold water, and have nobody to talk to but your horse. You would then come home and be happier about wearing dresses, marrying some chinless wonder from the lower aristocracy, and producing lots of children.'

Larissa's shoulders drooped. 'If my father were here now, I would . . .'

'Lady Larissa,' Winston interrupted. 'I know this is a delicate moment, but I don't suppose you saw what happened to a large dragon, a sinister sorceress, a bald wizard that you met briefly, three hundred other fat wizards that you never met, and an army that was with them?'

'The sorceress arrived as daylight was fading, just after you left,' said Larissa. 'I stayed hidden. I thought they might have been freebooters, seeking to catch me and hold me to ransom. The sorceress tied up the dragon with coils of glowing ropes that moved like snakes and burned anything they touched – except the dragon. They just entangled him like iron chains.'

'That's very potent magic!' exclaimed Winston. 'It should have drained and killed Yolantha many times over.'

'By the time the dragon was bound, about fifty of her wizards were really thin and drained of energy. Some even fainted.'

'It looks like she brought the wizards to fuel her casting powers, far beyond a human's ability. But wizards can't be strung together like that.'

She has the Imperium Key, said Elvar in Winston's mind. *It can allow her to do things like that.*

'I think I know why she needs a dragon,' said Winston.

'Why does who need a dragon?' asked Larissa.

Oh yes, said Elvar. *She will haul him back to Blackstone Mountain and make a new portal of him.*

'She means to turn him into another tower,' said Winston.

'Tower?' exclaimed Larissa.

'I'm talking to someone in my head,' said Winston. 'Go on, Elvar.'

Yes, it makes sense, said Elvar. *Open the portal to a dragon world, and she gets control of lots of energies from that world. She will soon rule this world, put the local dragons in their place, defeat the human armies, and unify the various wizard guilds under her own leadership. For her it may be a better outcome than gaining control of a portal to my iffryt world.*

'Please explain,' said Winston.

'Explain what?' Larissa asked.

Winston put a finger to his lips.

A summoned iffryt is basically a slave with very useful talents, said Elvar. *It has wings and can transform into various shapes when required, but can also bring a whole new type of magical power into the world.*

'Not good,' Winston concluded.

'What's not good?' asked Larissa.

'Remember the sorceress who defeated the

dragon? Imagine her with the energies of an entire dragon world to draw upon.'

Larissa nodded. She'd seen Yolantha in action. She knew that if the sorceress's powers were magnified any further, she would be unstoppable.

'Is there anything we can do, apart from hide?' she asked.

'I know where she's going,' said Winston. 'She'll go to Blackstone Mountain, it's at the junction of four very significant lines of influence.'

'I've heard of it,' said Larissa. 'Virtrian Hale, one of my father's ancestors, went there once on a quest. There's some sort of deadly tower on the peak, according to the family chronicle.'

'The tower's gone.'

'Gone? You mean it isn't still there?'

'Well . . . I broke it.'

'*You?* I don't believe you! That thing was more dangerous than a sky full of dragons. Hale's squire only found enough of him to fill a forage bag.'

We should go there and spy on what she is doing, suggested Elvar.

'It's a four-hundred-mile trek, and I'm very weak,' said Winston, reminding himself that

Larissa couldn't hear Elvar's voice. 'Besides, Yolantha will post guards all along the road with instructions to look out for someone who looks like me.'

Flying is out of the question, said Elvar. *One more transformation without weeks of rest and recovery will kill both of us.*

'Is there anything useful I can do?' asked Larissa.

'You, help me?' exclaimed Winston. 'Why?'

'I want to annoy my father.'

'You could do that more easily by offering him some dragon brain.'

'And I want to help with a real and important task.'

'When I need someone to get themselves killed for no sensible reason, you will be the first person I contact,' said Winston.

'I'm sick of being patronised!' shouted Larissa. 'If you're any sort of gentleman you will give me a chance.'

I hate to admit it, but she could be useful, said Elvar in Winston's mind. *You are far too weak to travel by yourself.*

'All right, all right, transport to Haldan would

be greatly appreciated,' said Winston aloud.

'Good. My horse can provide transport, but I would like to call in at Loseros first.'

Winston waited at the gate of the de Green mansion while Larissa went inside. He soon heard shouting, followed by the sound of glass and crockery smashing. Not long after that, Larissa emerged, slamming the gate behind her. She helped Winston back onto her horse and they set off along the street.

'Sounds like that could have gone better,' Winston commented.

'Patronising old wretches!' snapped Larissa.

'My father was worse, trust me on that subject.'

'Did you really conjure up a demon that force fed him dragon brain, then tried to drown him in the goldfish pond?'

'I think he was exaggerating.'

'He does that a lot. Well, I wish to join you on your quest!'

'You've done enough.'

'But I've just disowned my family.'

'Larissa, you can't help more than you already

have. I need to go on a long sea voyage to Grenwell, then travel south through the Harst Mountains to where Yolantha will try to rebuild the portal.'

'You're in no condition for such a long journey,' said Larissa.

'Neither are you! Who tried to fight a dragon two days ago? Who still has a wrenched shoulder and several dozen other injuries?'

'Then you shouldn't go either!'

'I *must* go, there's nobody else trying to stop Yolantha!' Winston insisted. 'She has hundreds of other wizards in her power. She would have had me as well if I hadn't deserted.'

'How will you pay for the voyage?'

'I have a sister who can get me onto a ship.'

'And after that?'

'I'll walk. I'm good at walking.'

'Winston, I collected my own savings after telling my father what I thought of him, throwing my mother's Varlin glassware collection at her, and then telling my sister that she can have the family name, mansion and fortune. We're going to do something heroic at Blackstone Mountain, and I'm going to pay whatever it costs to get us there.'

The bilge pipe incident happened while Griffid was being unloaded from the barges. Being designed for sacks of grain or barrels of ale, rather than Griffid's fifteen-ton weight, one of the cranes buckled, splintered, then came apart. The other two cranes were already near the limit of what they could lift, and the operators hurriedly cut their ropes. It was no particular problem for Griffid, whose nostrils were just above the water. But Faramond was in the dragon's cavernous mouth, holding on to one tombstone-sized tooth as the incoming stream of water threatened to sluice him into the dragon's stomach.

'Can it get any worse?' cried the wizard to no one in particular.

Oh yes it can, replied the dragon in his mind.

Griffid's jaws were now underwater. Faramond was tempted to scream, but holding his breath seemed like a better idea.

Ah, that Yolantha, she thinks of everything, said Griffid. *She's had her men fetch a length of bilge pipe. You do know what bilge water is, don't you? It builds up in the bottom of barges, and is pretty foul. Dead rats, mice, their droppings, rotting fish heads, and even the offerings of crewmen and passengers too modest to prop themselves over the side when nature calls. Ah yes, and here comes a pair of crewmen with a twin bellows bilge pump. Nothing but the best for Yolantha's dear friend Faramond.*

Faramond was on the verge of passing out when a pipe bubbling air was pushed between Griffid's teeth. In spite of what the dragon had told him about what normally travels through bilge pipes, Faramond had no hesitation when it came to choosing between putting the pipe in his mouth and drowning.

It was five hours before the broken crane was repaired and the docks' fourth crane was hauled into position. By then it was late in the day, and Yolantha decided to spend the night in Highport. Faramond could smell the pies and freshly baked bread from the dockside taverns.

'I won't be much good to Yolantha dead of starvation!' the wizard kept calling between Griffid's teeth.

Yolantha must have heard, because one of the carters pushed some thinly sliced bread and slivers of cheese into the dragon's mouth.

'Ya want some water, too?' asked the man. 'I got a pipe.'

'I think I've swallowed enough water for one day,' said Faramond. 'And I'm never going to put another pipe in my mouth as long as I live.'

The next morning Yolantha's strange caravan started out along the road into the mountains. In spite of his resolution, Faramond's stomach soon got the better of him, and he returned to drinking soup and water, sealed in sausage gut and passed between Griffid's teeth.

Having reached Haldan, Winston sought out the former slave wizard Stylan, who now had a shop near the waterfront. He agreed to look after Winston's books and Larissa's horse and armour. After buying Winston some travelling gear in the market, they made their way to the harbour. Stanni's ship happened to be tied up there, but the captain was planning to sail north across the Centralian Sea to Savaria. Larissa convinced him to call in at Grenwell first.

'Winston, do you realise that your lady paid the captain about half what the cargo is worth to divert to Grenwell?' said Stanni as the boat put to sea.

Larissa was at the stern, making sure that nobody in the pay of her parents was following them. Winston was at the bow, checking the boat's heading against the sun's position to make sure they were going in the right direction.

'Stanni, there's been a magical accident, and there are things I must do south of the Copperhead mines,' Winston explained to his sister. 'Larissa is . . . able to help.'

'She looks able, all right.'

'Aye.'

'So much so she could be an armed guard. She hit the midshipman and laid him out cold. Magnificent right cross. I saw it all.'

'He called her Seagull Larissa.'

'He did?' said Stanni. 'He's more of a fool than I gave him credit for.'

'She's very . . . determined. I saw her take on the dragon Griffid.'

'She did?'

'It's true, I swear it.'

'Ah, now I understand,' Stanni said, smirking. 'She's on some quest, and you're working for her as the hired brains.'

The voyage to Grenwell took a week, after which Larissa bought passage on a galley barge being rowed up the Icewater River. The river was navigable for the first two hundred miles, and after ten days the Harst Mountains were visible, rising from the plain ahead.

'According to the map, only seventy miles to go after Copperhead,' said Winston as he and Larissa sat at the bow of the barge.

'According to the barge master, we also have to travel three miles straight up, and you still have trouble walking the length of the barge.'

'I'm feeling stronger every day.'

'Winston, you're still less than half my weight,' Larissa pointed out.

'No I'm not.'

'I weigh a hundred and seventy pounds. I saw you checking your weight on the barge's cargo scales this morning. Eighty-two pounds is not a healthy weight for a fourteen-year-old boy.'

'Fifteen in five months.'

Larissa rolled her eyes. 'Tell me what to do at Blackstone Mountain. You can stay at Copperhead and I'll go on alone.'

'How are you on the theory and practice of Countercast magic?'

'I . . .' Larissa floundered.

'And your hunting skills?'

'I survived many weeks in Kalderial.'

'I spoke with the master of The Wayfarer's Boots, the inn a few miles out of the city. You returned there every night to eat and sleep.'

'Well, sometimes.'

'I have a bow and hunting arrows. Can you use them?'

'Yes.'

'Against live, moving targets the size of snow hares?'

'How hard can it be?'

'Harder than you think. Ever repaired an arrow that hit a rock instead of a rabbit?'

'I can learn.'

'Can you navigate by the sun and stars when there is no trail to follow? Larissa, you may be good at charging some armoured oick on horseback,' said Winston, 'but without me you'll not even reach the tower, let alone do anything useful if you do get there. We must both go.'

We are all going to die, said Elvar in the privacy of Winston's head, *but with luck she will die first.*

The barge could go no further than Copperhead Landing, which was where the copper ore was smelted before being shipped to the coast on barges. Here they bought all the cheese, sausage, dried fruit and trail biscuits that Larissa could carry. They then set off along the road to a copper mine further south and that led into the mountains. The road was wide enough for pony carts at first, and Winston spent a few coppers to ride in an empty cart going back up to the mine.

Larissa refused to ride in the cart.

'This is undignified,' she said. 'I'm from a noble family. I shouldn't be hauled about like a load of rocks. Knights only ride horses.'

'I won't tell anyone,' Winston replied.

'I'll know.'

'The mine's twenty-five miles further south and two miles upwards. After that it's another mile straight up, and forty-five more miles south before we reach Blackstone Mountain. Believe me, if it's possible to let a horse do the walking for you, do it. I've travelled a lot in the mountains. The air is thin, there's no such thing as a level road, and you get tired very quickly.'

'How long will it take to reach Blackstone Mountain?'

'Perhaps two months.'

Larissa was incredulous. 'Two months? Father says a soldier can march fifty miles in a day.'

'In mountains, with no trail, no supply wagons, no horses, no grazing even if you had a horse, and no wayside inns with cheery landlords and welcoming fires in the hearths? Two months is realistic.'

'But Winston, our food will be gone in two weeks.'

'Then we'll have to hunt.'

Larissa staggered, then collapsed after another five miles. When she regained consciousness, she was in the tray of the cart beside Winston.

'Thin air can sneak up and ambush you before you know it,' was all that he said.

At the copper mine, Winston and Larissa were able to buy more food and ask for directions, and the miners were very surprised to see them. The landlord of the shed that passed for a tavern told Winston of a steep path no more than inches wide that led further into the mountains, but said that, apart from a few shepherds and their flocks, they were at the end of the road. They set off after eating a lunch of stale bread, weak ale and the sludge that was in the pot over the tavern's fire.

'I fear that I'm sick,' said Larissa as they made camp at the end of the first day of actual trekking. 'I find it hard to draw breath and my strength is gone.'

'Mountain illness,' said Winston. 'Like I said, the air is thinner up here. We're lucky. In winter this place would be under deep snow. Once we get higher, there's snow on the ground even in summer, and there are no bushes to use for fires.'

'How do you know so much about everything?' asked Larissa.

'People love to talk about what they know best, so I just get them talking. That's how I learn. I know I have a lot to learn and I don't say much.'

'I must seem worse than useless to you,' Larissa admitted.

'No, you seem like a knight,' said Winston.

'That sounded more like an insult than a compliment.'

'It was an observation. Knights know warfare, and they have lots of people to help them get to battlefields without having to do things like chase dinner, wash clothes, pitch tents, make fires, sharpen swords and polish the armour. When there is no war to provide amusement, they just run their estates, stage feasts and fight in tournaments.'

Larissa thought about this while Winston showed her how to make a fire.

'The knights in the stories that the bards sing have adventures in distant lands,' she said at last.

'Those people are adventurers, the bards just call them knights to make them sound important,' said Winston. 'Oh, and here's another thing to remember. It gets very cold in mountains, and we have only two blankets and our trail cloaks to keep us warm. Leave your clothes and boots on while you sleep.'

'I've slept in my clothes before!' said Larissa.

'That's a step in the right direction.'

It's all the other steps that cause the grief, added Elvar in Winston's mind. *Can you go hunting – alone? We need to talk. Properly.*

There is only one thing that Larissa is good for, and that's money, said Elvar as Winston stalked what was probably a snow hare amid the rocks.

'She's tough and she's learning,' he replied.

That is the trouble, Winston. We need someone who already knows everything that you do.

'So far she hasn't slowed us down. She carries more of the gear and supplies than I do.'

Strong is not the same as tough. What happens in four or five weeks, when we are nowhere near Blackstone Mountain and the food runs out? She needs more food than you. She will weaken faster when the food runs out and the hunting fails.

'What are you getting at?'

You have to accept that before we reach Blackstone Mountain you will need to be strong enough to morph into me. You will have to leave the girl to starve and fly the remaining distance.

'You can fly back and save her after . . .'

After what? We are going to die because Yolantha has an army, a dragon and hundreds of wizards. We are going to die, and Larissa is going to die. At best we will die destroying Yolantha's dragon tower.

'What exactly are you saying?'

You have to tell yourself that Larissa is already dead. It will make it easier when you have to leave her.

Winston caught nothing that evening. When he returned to the camp, he showed Larissa how to cut bushes to cushion themselves as they slept. He also insisted that they keep their gear in the small tent.

'Shepherds wear sheepskin shoes because they're soft, warm and very quiet,' he explained. 'They're ideal for sneaking up on sleeping travellers and slinking off with whatever's not in the tent.'

Once they were in the tent and trying to sleep, Larissa had her last lesson for the day.

'I'm freezing!' she stammered through chattering teeth after fifteen minutes. 'Two blankets and a rain cloak each isn't enough. We need to return to the mine and buy more.'

'One last lesson in travel survival for the day,' said Winston. 'Tonight, you're not tired enough to ignore the cold, so you'll lie awake. Tomorrow night you'll be truly exhausted, and sleep will claim you.'

Yolantha had gathered three hundred and thirty-six wizards at Blackstone Mountain. Scattered about the base were a hundred carters, a thousand mercenaries, and several hundred other people to prepare meals, fetch water, tend fires and carry away the nightsoil. The sorceress had in effect established a small town in the wilderness, and it had a single purpose: to get Griffid to the top of Blackstone Mountain.

The dragon was hauled off the six carts that had carried him all the way from Highport, then bound upright in a sitting position, with his tail curled around his feet and his snout pointed straight up in the air. Faramond had been provided with a rope to make a harness, and now he was dangling above the chasm that was the dragon's throat with the harness tethered to one of the massive teeth that imprisoned him.

Yolantha climbed up along the ridges that ran along the creature's back and neck, stopping on his snout. She gazed at the circle of wizards below.

'It's a law of enchantment that a wizard cannot levitate anything that they cannot carry with their physical body,' she said. 'Did you know that, Faramond? Probably not. I have enough wizards to carry a fifteen-ton dragon. Levitating the same dragon to the peak of Blackstone Mountain is like each of them carrying a hundred-pound pack the same distance. Difficult, but not impossible.'

I would eat you, except that I don't want to poison myself, growled Griffid.

'And your jaws are bound shut. Let us begin.'

Yolantha extended her arms to the side, then raised them to the sky. Slowly, at the pace of a single wizard climbing the steps of Blackstone Mountain with a hundred-pound pack, the dragon Griffid rose into the air.

By counting steps Winston estimated that they were managing to travel a little less than a mile a day, on average. Larissa practised with Winston's bow, and turned out to be quite a good shot once she learned to aim a little ahead of whatever moving target she hoped to eat. She learned to navigate by the sun and stars, and realised that it was not as hard as her father had told her. Cooking was even easier. Winston's skills with meals consisted of throwing chopped-up pieces of everything into a pot, adding water, and putting the pot over a fire. They had no pot, so when they caught the occasional rabbit or bird, Larissa learned that spit-roasting meat over a fire was no great challenge.

It was already autumn, but there were still shepherds about with their flocks of sheep and goats. From them they bought dried and smoked meat, and more fleece. They were told about trails leading even further south, trails not known to the tavern's landlord back at the copper mine. Presently the mountains became steeper, and there were no more bushes to provide firewood. There was no more grass, either. That meant there were no more shepherds, sheep, goats or rabbits.

'What was it like for you in Loseros?' Larissa asked one night as she and Winston huddled under their sheepskins in the tent.

'You lived there, too,' said Winston.

'I lived on Mansion Hill, although it will soon be Mansion Island with the sea rising. What was it like where you lived? I mean, how did you and your sisters grow up to be so tough?'

'What do you call an innocent, caring child in Loseros?'

'I'm not very good at—'

'Dead.'

'Oh. But what about the militia patrols?'

'The people who live on Mansion Hill pay for them, so they patrol Mansion Hill. Where I grew up, we had no militia patrols.'

Larissa thought about this for a long time. Some of the fundamentals in her life were no longer feeling quite so fundamental. It was a bitterly cold night, and Winston lay awake, fantasising about extra warmth.

'Your teeth are chattering,' said Larissa in the darkness.

'They're trying to keep warm.'

'Mine are, too.'

'Must be because they're cold.'

'I'm very cold. And tired. It gets worse every

day, and . . . I've been thinking. You may have to leave me tomorrow and go on alone.'

Don't listen to her, Winston, said Elvar. *She's just trying to make you think she's being noble so you will be sympathetic and stay with her.*

'I mean, we are both going to die at Blackstone Mountain, so does it really matter if I die here instead?' Larissa continued.

I knew she was going to say that! shouted Elvar in Winston's head.

'I'm getting really sick of this!' Winston snapped.

'I'm sick of being cold, too,' said Larissa.

She wants you to put your arms around her, Winston! Don't do it!

'You're jealous!' he shouted, sitting up abruptly.

Larissa frowned. 'Jealous of who?'

Don't be a fool! I'm not jealous, I'm not even human.

'Well, if you're so good at being clever and knowing what to do, *you* do something, instead of yelling in my head!'

Winston crawled out of the tent and stood up. There was bright moonlight but no wind as he traced the spell.

Winston, stop, this is not yet a good time to—

'Iffryt!' called Winston, then clapped.

Larissa put her head out of the tent in time to see him morph into the thing that had forced her father to eat a bag of dragon brain.

'The demon!' she shrieked. '*You* are the demon!'

'Oh, give it a rest,' muttered Elvar as she slumped down onto a rock with her head in her wing claws.

Well? asked Winston in Elvar's head. *Now what?*

'Oh, shut up, Winston Spellwyn.'

'Winston?' gasped Larissa. 'Where is he?'

'In my head. Only I can hear him.'

'You mean Winston is half a demon?'

'I am an iffryt. Winston and I share the same . . . substantial manifestation of . . . Oh, what is the use, I'm not even sure that I understand what we are.'

'So you're a girl?'

'I am a female iffryt and not what you could call a girl.'

'And where have you been all this time?'

'In Winston's head.'

'Seeing and hearing everything?'

'Yes.'

'Poor boy. No wonder he was always so chivalrous toward me.'

'I think he would have been chivalrous even without me inside his head.'

There was an extended silence. Eventually, Larissa remembered her manners. 'You should come back into the tent,' she said. 'It's numbingly cold out here.'

Elvar was too drained from the transformation to refuse. Very soon, her far higher body temperature made conditions a lot warmer inside the tent.

'Winston's inside your head now?' asked Larissa.

'He certainly is, so be careful what you say.'

This is wonderful, said Winston. *I don't feel hungry any more, and it's nice and warm.*

'Oh, shut up!' snapped Elvar.

'Were you speaking to Winston?' asked Larissa.

'Who else?'

It clouded over and snowed for the first time during the night, but the sky had cleared by morning. The sunrise was blood red and radiating little warmth.

Larissa looked worried. 'Why does the sky look like that?'

'A volcano somewhere has been blowing dust and muck into the air,' replied Elvar, sounding reassuringly unconcerned.

'Isn't a red sky in the morning some sort of warning for shepherds?' asked Larissa.

'Could be, but when the sky goes as red as that it is usually a volcano.'

It turned out that the transformation into Elvar's true form actually saved Larissa's life. She was too heavy for the weakened Elvar to fly with, but by grasping Larissa by the shoulders, Elvar could glide across chasms and valleys that would have been difficult to cross on foot. She could also hunt wildlife from the air. Although Larissa drew the line at eating raw flesh, it meant that the young warrior could have all their supplies, while Elvar ate what she had caught and killed. Because of Elvar's body temperature, Larissa was able to sleep soundly in the much warmer tent.

See that ridge in the distance? said Winston one evening as Larissa was putting up the tent. *The one that looks like the teeth of a saw?*

'Yes,' said Elvar.

'Are you speaking to Winston?' asked Larissa.

'I am, just ignore me.'

I've seen that ridge from the other side, continued Winston. *It's the watershed of the Harst Mountains. That means the Icewater River is fed from this side and the Harst River from the southern side. It also means we're only five miles from Blackstone Mountain.*

'We could be there tomorrow if we abandon our camping gear and supplies, and I fly with Larissa.'

'Could be where?' asked Larissa.

'Blackstone Mountain,' replied Elvar. 'How do you feel about dying horribly with me tomorrow?'

For several days Griffid had been slowly transforming into a tower. His feet, tail and lower body were already stone blocks, but the rest of him was still dragon.

'I can't even remember my last meal,' whimpered Faramond, still hanging in his harness above Griffid's long, deep throat.

I can, and it was you, replied Griffid.

'How was I to know that Yolantha cast an entanglement spell upon me?'

Because you are a wizard and should know an entanglement spell when you see one.

'I was blindfolded.'

Lies. If the entanglement spell binding my jaws is ever released, I will eat you.

The dragon's forked tongue rose out of the depths below and rubbed against the wizard. Normally Faramond would have screamed, but by now he was almost beyond caring.

Actually, you taste pretty repulsive. I think I'll just flame you.

'Alas, what will become of me?' moaned Faramond.

Can you look upward, between my teeth?

'Yes. I see a disk of, well, nothingness. It's like a patch of night in the blue sky.'

That, my obnoxious and greedy lunch, is a portal to another place. I am being built into a tower that will eventually enclose it, and it will channel limitless magic into this world. However, the theory has a tiny flaw—

'Damn the theory, what will happen to me?'

You will be turned to stone and become part of the tower. Perhaps as some kind of useless decoration, like a bloated gargoyle. Just imagine, no more worrying about where your next meal is coming from, ever again.

———◆———

By the time they'd finally reached Blackstone Mountain, Winston had counted a hundred and five days since they'd set out from Kalderial. From one of the outcrops surrounding the thin spire of black stone, they saw that the area at its base had been turned into a vast campsite.

Most of the warriors were divided between guarding the road leading south to the Harst River, and the main trail running through the mountains. The wizards that Yolantha had gathered together were sitting in a circle near the base of the small, thin mountain. They were not yet emaciated, but they were definitely looking thinner. Silvery threads that glowed as brightly as lightning from a storm linked them to one another. Directly above them, and nearly level with the peak, Griffid was floating beside the mountain. He too was bound by silvery threads.

'The dragon is flying, yet his wings are bound,'

said Larissa, peering through the farsight tube she had stolen from her father.

'No, the wizards are levitating him,' said Elvar. 'He weighs fifteen tons, so the combined power of over three hundred wizards is needed to support him. The Imperium Key allows Yolantha to link wizards together like that. She will be somewhere down there, directing them.'

'I see someone standing alone at the centre of the circle of magicians.'

'That will be her.'

Larissa watched as Griffid rose level with the peak of Blackstone Mountain, then moved sideways and descended. Now his bonds pulled at him to stretch him upwards, and a black disk formed just above his head. Around his feet, the beginnings of a circular tower were forming. His tail had already dissolved.

'I can see through the dragon,' said Larissa. 'Fill a bottle with smoke and that's what he's becoming.'

'I see a dark disk,' said Elvar. 'He's becoming the living gateway to another world.'

'Poor thing, I almost feel sorry for him.'

'You tried to kill him!' exclaimed Elvar.

'Big mistake. Can we save him?'

'Probably not,' said Elvar. 'So we're back to dying to save this world. The disk is a portal, already reaching into another world.'

'Even though Yolantha hasn't finished building her tower?' asked Larissa.

'Yes, but it isn't safe. Imagine a bridge that is only partially built. It looks like a bridge, but most of the things that make it strong have not been added yet. What happens if some clown comes along with a dozen oxen pulling, a wagon loaded with heavy stones?'

'It collapses,' said Larissa. 'Is that what we have to do?'

'You can't do anything more,' said Elvar. 'I hate to say it, but thank you for helping to get us here.'

'Gracious of you,' replied Larissa, raising the farsight tube again. 'There's no door at the base of the new tower.'

'Yolantha is taking no chances,' said Elvar. 'When finished, it will have no door, windows or arrow slits. Not even airy balconies with a nice view of the sunset behind the other mountains. This is the best and only time for us to attack.'

The word *attack* had been spoken. Larissa felt her pulse quicken.

'I can help with attacking!'

Elvar shook her head. 'I shall fly for the tower and try to drop through the portal. That will cause it to collapse.'

And kill Griffid? asked Winston.

'Griffid is the bridge, we are the cart full of stones. We both get washed away into the dragon world.'

'Might you survive in the dragon world?' asked Larissa.

'If it is anything like my world, perhaps,' said Elvar.

'What is your world like?'

'There is a huge red sun that always sits on the horizon. Most of my world is too hot or too cold, but we iffryts live in a narrow width of forest that circles it.'

'Circles a *globe* world?' exclaimed Larissa.

'Yes.'

'Why don't your people fall off the bottom of it?'

'The same reason that your people don't fall off this world.'

'But our world is the top of the World Dragon's head. Each day she breathes a fireball that is the sun, and the moon is her egg which will hatch in ten thousand years.'

'So you think humans live on the World Dragon's head, like little insects?' asked Elvar.

'Well, we like to think of ourselves as servants that she created to—'

'Never mind. What would happen if humans tunnelled deep enough to reach her brain?'

'I'm not sure,' said Larissa, who had never concerned herself with astronomy, geology or theology. 'I suppose the World Dragon would die, her head would tip over and we would fall off. Oh, and there would be no more suns, so we would freeze, too.'

'Really!' exclaimed Elvar.

Winston had not given much thought to the World Dragon. The world was there, so why worry about what held it up? Now there was a real prospect of paying her a visit, however, so he decided that it could be a good time to sort out his beliefs.

I try to keep an open mind, he said to Elvar.

'Good, you may soon have your mind expanded,' said Elvar.

What do you mean?

'I prefer to show rather than tell. Getting back to our plan of attack, Yolantha is sure to have defences, but I see none. That worries me. She must suspect that other dragons may hear about what she is doing to Griffid, and try to rescue him.'

Griffid is not a popular dragon, said Winston.

'True, and I see no dragons flying to the rescue, so it is up to us. What we need is a distraction.'

'I can provide a distraction!' said Larissa.

Elvar thought about this for a moment.

'I suppose you can indeed. Heave a few heavy rocks down a loose slope, start an avalanche, then run and hide. Yes, I like that idea.'

'Then I should say my goodbyes and get to work,' said Larissa.

With that she seized Elvar and hugged her with the awkwardness of someone who has never hugged anyone before, human or iffryt, then hurried away.

'What is Larissa doing? She has not started the avalanche yet,' Elvar said impatiently. 'How hard can it be to toss a few rocks down a mountain?'

Do you think we will see the World Dragon's brain when we fall through the portal? asked Winston.

'If we get in, no, but we may see something that would make priests, theologians and wizards very upset. Brace yourself, Winston. We are about to do something stupidly dangerous, then we shall do something insanely dangerous. I wonder what defences Yolantha has set up around Griffid and the portal.'

Chapter Nine

Nobody in Yolantha's camp was expecting a mundane attack from the north. The road south was heavily guarded, but the general security of the place was quite relaxed. The warriors who were off duty were watching in fascination as Griffid turned into a portal to another world, so it was not hard for Larissa to surprise one of them. Dressed in his cloak and some of his armour, she fitted right in. So disguised, she was able to secure herself a horse and lance. She already had a sword.

There were few mounted guardsmen or foot soldiers guarding the circle of gaunt and haggard wizards, linked together and centred on Yolantha. Larissa pulled back on the reins until her horse reared. This had no practical purpose, and although she told herself that it was to get Yolantha's attention, she secretly hoped that someone present with artistic skills would paint an inspiring, heroic picture of her on the rearing horse when it was all over. She then lowered her lance and charged. From high above, Elvar and Winston looked on in disbelief.

'Do you think she's ever had the term "certain death" explained to her?' asked Elvar.

Is that like what we're about to do? asked Winston.

'More or less. Time for us to die heroically.'

Elvar launched herself off the outcrop. Nobody below noticed.

One of the mounted warriors on patrol at the edge of Yolantha's circle of wizards made the mistake of drawing his sword and shouting at Larissa to stop, or he would kill her. She managed to put her lance through his chest before it snapped. The warrior flew backwards, screaming every second of his remaining life.

A ripple of movement snagged the line of magicians, but none dared break their magical chain in fear of Yolantha's wrath.

Larissa hastily flung the broken lance to the ground and drew her sword. She then aimed at the gap between two of the wizards linked by Yolantha's brightly glowing cables. The cables were stronger than they appeared, yet not strong enough. They entangled the legs of her horse, bringing it down, but snapped in the process of doing so. Larissa got up and brandished her sword, just as a wizard tried to grab her from behind. Her elbow slammed backwards into his head, then she removed the head of another wizard, who was tracing a spell. Screaming, she charged Yolantha, who had by now conjured a ball of writhing, golden cords. This she flung at Larissa, who collapsed in a tangle of gold.

As distractions went, it certainly got the job done.

She's sure to be dead by now, said Winston as Elvar flew for the incomplete dragon tower.

'Odds of twelve dozen to one, sure to be,' Elvar replied. 'I told her that we only needed an avalanche, even a small one. Just a loud enough rock fall would have done.'

They circled ever closer to Blackstone Mountain, yet whatever guardians Yolantha may have put around it weren't attacking. Nor had they hit any invisible wall.

'I need to gain height, to get above the disk,' said Elvar.

You mean that dark, swirly thing at the top of the tower that Griffid's becoming?

'Yes.'

It's not like the other disk.

'That's because it's not yet working properly.'

Will we kill the World Dragon when we fly into its brain?

'We are not flying into any dragon's brain. We are going to fly into the portal and make it fall apart.'

And there's a huge brain down there.

'Winston, stop that or I'll agree with Faramond and call you an idiot! There's another world beyond the portal, a world of dragons. With luck, they will think we are cute and keep us as a pet.'

Winston gulped mentally. *The portal gets destroyed and we get marooned on the other world? If it exists?*

'Better than being dead.'

Says who?

A great spiralling, buffeting wind wrenched at Elvar, tossing her about and nearly breaking her wings.

'Yolantha's defences!' she shouted. 'Exclusion spell! I expected something like it. It is meant to keep away birds, bats and wizards on flying rugs!'

What do we do?

'Make ourselves invisible to the spell.'

As soon as she was far enough away from the tower to be out of the spell's reach, Elvar turned back and gained height, heading out over the portal. When she folded her wings, she dropped like a stone.

This won't work! cried Winston in her head as she plummeted. *I know this spell; it will exclude all things that are capable of flying, whether they're using their wings or not.*

'But you are not capable of flying,' said Elvar, tracing a spell with her wing claw.

Elvar spoke the word of transformation and morphed back into Winston.

'Elvar, what do you think you're *doing?*' screamed Winston, grabbing at handfuls of air as he dropped toward the portal.

You *have no wings, so the exclusion spell cannot affect you as you fall.*

As Elvar had hoped, no wind sprang up to blow Winston away from the portal because he wasn't a bird or bat or riding a flying device. He plunged into the portal, and as he fell the opening collapsed behind him, but not before Griffid appeared.

For Faramond, the collapse of the tower was rather like an individual soldier's view of a battle. He was more or less aware of what was going on around him, but didn't have an overview, like a commander looking down from a strategic hill.

It's a well-known property of magical portals that objects are only ever drawn through whole, otherwise they would be shredded. The portal descended until it touched Griffid's upturned snout. It also touched the casting binding his jaws shut, then continued its descent, passing over the entire casting, which vanished into the portal. Realising that his jaws were free, Griffid opened them wide and drew breath to burn Faramond into a cloud of smoke with suggestions of burnt fat. Faramond had been faster, however, and scrambled out of his harness and down to the ridge along the back of Griffid's neck. More of

Yolantha's binding enchantments were lower down and still intact, so that all the dragon could do was spray flames about, thinking that he was burning Faramond.

The wizard made his way down the dragon's neck and back, using the dragon's rippled ridge like a ladder, then jumped the last few feet to the ground that supported the half-dragon, half-tower Griffid. He made for the steps that wound around the mountain, then paused on the first step and looked up.

As the portal disk swept down over Griffid, the dragon's lower body transformed from stone blocks back into scales, spines, tail, feet and wings. The golden enchanted bonds holding Griffid were swallowed by the portal, leaving the enormous creature free to fly away. Then he looked down and saw a petrified Faramond gazing up at him.

You! Still alive! roared Griffid in Faramond's head. He drew breath for another blast of searing flame.

Hesitating to incinerate Faramond for that moment was Griffid's mistake. Just then the descending portal reached the rock at the peak of Blackstone Mountain only inches from where Faramond was standing. There was a blinding flash of yellow light, as intense as the sun. Then the portal vanished, taking Griffid with it. The top of Blackstone Mountain was once again bare, solid rock.

'What an absolute wonder,' said Faramond as he began the long descent. 'I survived all that without so much as a scratch.'

Within moments, Winston was in complete darkness. He was fairly sure that he was falling, but no air was rushing past and there was no sensation of speed. Above them was a yellowish light, accompanied by crackling discharges, like a thunderstorm being forced down a long tunnel.

'I'd really like to know what's going on, even if I'd rather not know,' said Winston, almost too exhausted from the transformation to care about how he was about to die.

We are falling through a tunnel in your world that does not exist, said Elvar. *It does not exist in the other world, either. We are in a bubble of air about six feet in diameter, and that should be enough.*

'Enough for what?'

Enough to keep you alive for the three quarters of an hour that it takes to fall through a world.

'Why don't I weigh anything?'

Because Wilderclaw's Second Law of Relative Motion states that a body within a freely falling body will be denied the influence of gravity.

'What's gravity?'

Too hard to explain. You weigh nothing just now, so live with it.

Convinced that he was about to die, and quite probably take the World Dragon with him, Winston tried to think of something pleasant. He tried food, but he wasn't an expert on the topic. Faramond always bagged the best pickings. He had never tasted wine, and the ale that everyone drank in preference to well water was bland and almost tasteless. Girls should have been a reliable topic, but working for Faramond meant living in a ruined city, where the company was one male wizard and one male dragon. He thought of holding hands with Elvar when they had first approached Blackstone Tower.

'Why is so much fuss made about holding hands and kissing?' he wondered aloud.

Can you repeat the question? asked Elvar.

'Kissing and holding hands, why are they so special?'

We're falling through a portal between worlds and you want to discuss the theory of romance?

'I've never been kissed; my family isn't big on displays of emotion. Now I'll never find out what it's like to kiss a girl.'

You're not going to die, we're just going to a dragon world.

'Well, you can't expect me to kiss a dragon! What's kissing like?'

Winston, kissing is one of those things you have to do for yourself before you can talk about it properly.

'I gather you've never kissed anyone, either?'

No! I am an iffryt and I have spent a lot of time in a glass jar.

'But before that? Don't iffryts kiss each other?'

No.

Winston gave up and began to count heartbeats instead.

In the light coming from the collapsing portal behind them, Winston saw patterns and layers in the rocks flashing past. *Most likely they're the structure of the World Dragon's skull*, he decided. *What should a dragon's brain look like? Not like the green plant I cut for Larissa's father.* Winston concentrated on counting again. He had reached a thousand when the tunnel ahead and below them brightened.

'Tell me that's not the World Dragon's brain,' said Winston.

It's not the World Dragon's brain, Elvar assured him.

'But it is, isn't it?'

Winston, your world is a ball of rock surrounded by air and water. At the centre is an area where the rock is so hot that it is liquid. Where do you think volcanoes come from?

'Faramond says volcanoes are fire leaking through the World Dragon's sinuses when she breathes the fireball that becomes the next day's sun.'

Winston, do you believe anything else that Faramond says?

'Well, no.'

Then don't believe him about this.

Winston wasn't sure whether he felt worse about falling into the brain of the World Dragon and destroying the world, or emerging from the bottom of a sphere of rock and flying off into the sky forever. There was a third possibility, that of emerging from the bottom of the World Dragon's head, but that outcome was about as bad as the second possibility. By now the light was so intense that he had to shield his eyes with his hands, but even through his flesh, the brightness was unbearable. He started counting heartbeats again, as it kept his mind off where he was and what was happening to him. The light started to fade, and by the time he lowered his hands and opened his eyes, they were in darkness again, lit only by whatever was following them.

Faramond had only just started down the steps that wound around Blackstone Mountain when a powerful vortex wind plucked him up and flung him into clear air. What happened next was not because Faramond was a coward – he was – but when put under the most extreme stress the human body will say to itself: 'Bladder control, who needs it? I have to put all my concentration into staying alive.'

Trailing a stream of pee, Faramond did

indeed remember a spell that Winston had told him, a spell to transform one's clothing into what he called an air net. It was just the thing to slow oneself down when falling from a great height. Faramond traced the spell and cast the enchantment. His robe, trail cloak, sailor's trousers and boots were immediately changed into a billowing half-sphere of cloth. Unfortunately for Faramond, he had forgotten that the idea was to hold onto it. The cloth was ripped out of his hands by the air rushing past and reverted to a robe.

As the ground rushed up, Faramond resigned himself to going wherever he was going to go in the afterlife . . . and then he stopped falling three inches before impact. The contents of his bladder caught up with him and pattered down onto his body like yellow rain. Yolantha stood close by, arms folded and shaking her head. With a snap of her fingers, she broke the spell that had saved Faramond's life and he fell the last three inches to the ground. His robe, cloak, trousers and boots landed nearby.

'Get to your feet, get dressed,' commanded Yolantha. 'I have a question for you. Actually, I have quite a lot of questions for you – and for her.'

Nearby, a bruised and bleeding girl was being extracted from her armour by Yolantha's mercenaries.

'Put them in that little cave at the base of the mountain and guard them until I'm ready to interrogate them.'

'You can't lock me away with *him*!' shouted Larissa.

'Yes, I can. Try not to kill him.'

Winston had counted to a thousand again by the time the darkness ahead of them started giving way to a blue brightness. This was shaping up to be the most profound moment in his short life. If the World Dragon existed, they were about to emerge from the bottom of her head. Blue brightness meant sky. It had been late afternoon when they dropped into the portal, so it would be morning on the other side of the world. The bottom side. The side that everything would fall off into the sky. The side that *he* would fall off.

'There's light up ahead,' he muttered softly,

then wondered if he should try to think of some more significant last words.

We will have to become me again, as we may need wings, said Elvar. *We entered through a portal in the mountains, so we will probably emerge from a portal far above the level of most land.*

'Most land? In the other world? The dragon world?'

Yes. We shall emerge in the other world at the same height above sea level.

'And?'

If we stay you, we have no wings, so we start falling. Below us, the portal will seal itself shut. Then we stop, quite abruptly.

By now, Winston was in daylight, and several thousand feet above what looked like a city on a coast. The bubble of nothingness that had protected him vanished, and he began to fall.

Now do you believe in gravity? asked Elvar.

'Yes! Yes! Yes!'

Best you transform back into me, then!

'We've done two morphings in less than an hour. A third may kill us.'

Falling a couple of miles onto that city below us is even more likely to kill us. Transform! Now!

Winston traced the spell and spoke the word for iffryt, then finally morphed back into Elvar after flickering through several false starts. She wearily spread her wings and glided in a great circle to get a sense of where she was.

I see no tower down there, said Winston.

'Why should you? This is just the portal's exit, and we're still on your world.'

Was that meant to make sense?

'To me, yes.'

How do you know this isn't a dragon world?

'Dragons don't build cities, and we are above a city. That means we are on the opposite side of your world, which is a ball of rock that pulls everything on the surface in the direction of the centre. There is no world dragon.'

But why aren't we in a dragon world?

'Because apparently dragons come from this world, not some other.'

I gather I don't have to explain to Mum that I killed the World Dragon?

'No, but you might like to explain that it doesn't exist.'

Elvar was glancing about for the portal. She felt a pang of disappointment to see that it was still there, floating above the city.

'Looks like we failed,' she said, disheartened. At that moment Griffid emerged, fully formed as a dragon. The portal winked out of existence.

The yellow light behind us, it must have been Griffid! said Winston.

Griffid spread his wings, bellowed with anger, blew flame, and looked down at the city.

This is going to get ugly, said Winston.

'Why?' asked Elvar.

I know where we are! The fabled city of Havenport has a vast circular harbour with an island in the middle. Havenport is said to be the biggest slave market of all. It's so far away that it's only known of from legends and sailors' songs.

'The island is mostly a palace,' said Elvar.

Yes. The sailors say that it's the world's most beautiful palace, but it's surrounded by a city that is the very symbol of squalor and misery . . . and Griffid is diving for it.

'Is this significant?'

Yes! He's just spent over a hundred days as Yolantha's captive, so he's probably a bit sensitive on the subject of slavery.

A deluge of flame from Griffid's gaping mouth burst over the spires, domes and pleasure gardens of Havenport's royal palace. The dragon proceeded to circle the island, burning the royal barges and guard galleys, then did a tour of the entire circular harbour, burning every ship moored there. He returned to the palace and tore at the delicate marble walls with razor-sharp talons, before pouring yet more fire into the ruins. Satisfied at last, if not really happy, he curled up and went to sleep on what was left of the Tower of Stepped Gardens.

Elvar circled the island, buoyed by the updrafts from the fires.

'He seemed a bit cross,' she observed.

I noticed, Winston replied.

'Evidently, dragons are endemic to your world.'

Endemic?

'It means they've always lived here. Yolantha tried to open a portal to a dragon world by using a dragon to fashion the portal. Because dragons come from your world in the first place, her portal just led to the other side.'

I can't wait to get home!

'Ah, but we're twelve thousand miles away. Griffid fell through behind us when we collapsed the portal. Now we need to fly home to Dravinia.'

How far is twelve thousand miles? asked Winston.

'You would take three years to walk the distance – if you had a good, straight road, and someone leaving meals for you, and bridges over all the wet bits called oceans.'

Where do we start?

'Much to my surprise I'm alive, but my body feels about as strong as a boned fish. Once I've had a few days of rest and a lot of nourishing food, we fly. I can fly at the speed of a galloping horse, which is about thirty miles in the hour. At twelve hours flying in a day, that's over three hundred miles.'

But a day is twice as long as that.

'And I need to sleep, and hunt, then eat what I catch. Remember, I don't get energy by magic any more. I don't fly in rainstorms, either. They're cold and depressing, I can't navigate if I can't see the sun or stars, and I don't like having wet fur. That means forty days minimum to return, fifty to be on the safe side.'

Fifty days! That's nearly two months.

'True, but Yolantha will not be expecting us.'

Yolantha? You want to go back to her?

'Yes. She has the Imperium Key and can do a lot of damage with it. I have a plan to get it back from her.'

Involving me?

'Winston, everything I do has to involve you. We share the same body, remember?'

As if I could forget.

By now they had glided low enough to see that people in the city were looking upwards and pointing at them. Nobody was shooting anything in their direction, which was encouraging.

I wonder how Larissa died, said Winston.

'She died heroically, which is probably all she ever wanted.'

When we get back, I'll write an epic about how she died.

'Why?'

So people will remember her.

'She won't care. She's dead.'

Well, I care! I'm going to write one anyway.

'Stupid human.'

Heartless iffryt.

'I've got two hearts.'

Elvar descended even further, still circling the city.

'Strange, I see fires starting in parts of the city that Griffid didn't fly over,' said Elvar.

That will be the slaves negotiating with their masters about pay and conditions, said Winston. *Do you think someone will give us a map if you land? We need to plan our journey home while you rest.*

'Will we be welcome?'

You're vaguely dragon-shaped, except for the red fur, pointed ears, and a long, fluffy tail. A large dragon is curled up in the ruins of the palace, and that dragon just ended five thousand years of slavery in five minutes. Aye, I think someone who looks like Griffid's apprentice or daughter would be welcome down there.

Elvar landed amid what used to be the genteel mansions of the city, which meant that they belonged to those who had prospered most from the slave trade. A lot of people in expensive and well-tailored robes lay dead in the street, and former slaves were working their way through the former slave owners who were still alive. Elvar held out her wings for a moment. Everyone – former slaves and former slave masters alike – got to their knees and bowed until their foreheads touched the ground.

'Now what?' asked Elvar.

Say 'Aspir dar!' said Winston.

'What does that mean?' asked Elvar.

It's Sea Merchant, the trade language of sailors. It means 'stand up'.

Elvar spoke the words. Everyone obeyed.

I wonder if anyone speaks Dravinian? said Winston.

'Dravinian?' called Elvar.

'I am from the continent Dravinia,' called a female voice.

Elvar beckoned to her with a wing to approach. The girl was about twenty and had the body of a dancer. In her hand was a sword that had recently seen action.

'Your name?' Elvar asked.

'Preda, from Grenwell. Are you a servant of the dragon?'

'More or less. I don't suppose I could get something to eat? The past few hours have been quite a strain.'

'What do you eat?'

'Rats and mice,' said Elvar.

No! No! No! wailed Winston.

'Rabbits, pigeons and seagulls, if I have to,' Elvar amended, mocking Winston. 'Fish, if there's nothing else.'

'Then come this way.'

Winston whimpered quietly.

'Please, can you fetch a cart? I am very tired.'

Preda had a cart brought to Elvar, then took her to one of the mansions that hadn't yet been set on fire. They had to wait while former slaves removed several bodies and cleaned up pools of blood. A selection of rats and mice was brought out for her. A dozen or so young women stood in the background, cleaning their weapons and generally being vigilant.

'You seem to have military training,' said Elvar.

'I am what they call an "arena girl". We fight each other for the entertainment of our masters.'

'Your dead masters.'

Apart from Larissa, Winston had never encountered a real female warrior in his entire life. Now, he and Elvar were being waited upon by several dozen of them. The sight of plates of dead rats for the iffryt made Winston squirm, but Elvar preened.

Thousands of young male slaves were waiting outside, wanting to know if the dragon princess was recruiting for an army to march on other slave cities.

'I will need a pack that will strap firmly to my back,' said Elvar, once she had eaten her fill. 'Cram it with as many smoked rats as will fit into it.'

'Is something the matter?' asked Preda. 'Have we offended you?'

'No, but I can only stay for a few days while I rest.'

'But we would like you to stay here always, and rule us.'

'I don't do ruling.'

'Guide us, then.'

'If you put me in charge, you will always think of yourselves as slaves, and this day will just be thought of as a change of slave masters. Learn to govern yourselves.'

'But we have no experience with ruling.'

'*Psst!* Have you not noticed? Slaves run everything. All you have to do is delegate people to give the orders.'

'But they may become tyrants.'

'Then kill them. Now can I have a look at your very best maps?'

It was evening by the time Elvar felt well enough to fly out to the smoking ruins on the island. She landed beside Griffid's head.

Go away, he rumbled, without opening his eyes.

'I am Elvar.'

Pleased to meet you, now go away.

'What are your plans for the city?'

Are the slaves free?

'Yes, but their former owners are in reduced circumstances. Those who are still alive, anyway.'

Good.

'So you are not going to burn anything else?'

No.

'Or eat anyone?'

No.

'Well then, what next?'

I fly back to Dravinia and burn the sorceress Yolantha

into a pile of ash. Then . . . I just may return here. I like ruins.

'You certainly made a ruin of this palace. So that is all?'

Yes. How did I get to Havenport?

'Yolantha opened a portal to the opposite side of your world. I freed you by making you fall through it.'

But we live on a crown worn by the World Dragon.

'Wrong, but I am not going to argue. Take my word on it. If you just fly west for long enough, you will come to the same side of the world as Blackstone Tower, but in the southern hemisphere.'

Then how do I get to Blackstone Tower and kill Yolantha?

'Fly north.'

What was the fate of Winston?

'He's safe.'

And the warrior girl?

'She's dead.'

Not surprised. She was stupid enough to attack me with a lance.

'You owe me a very substantial favour. I set you free.'

Then ask.

'Promise not to harm anyone else in the city.'

They are fellow slaves, why should I hurt them?

Satisfied all would be fine, Elvar flew back to the docks area, where she set about memorising maps of the seaways and continents all the way to Dravinia.

Why do you want to bother with maps? asked Winston. *Don't you just fly west to the other side of the world, then fly north?*

'Without maps, how will we know when we are on the other side of the world? Dravinia is in the northern hemisphere. If we passed through the centre of the world, we are now in the southern hemisphere. What is in the southern hemisphere below Dravinia, Winston?'

I don't know.

'Then it's lucky I memorised the maps. If you must know, when we reach five volcanic islands forming a circle about a hundred miles across, we will be on the exact opposite side of the world and have to turn due north.'

Yolantha sealed Larissa and Faramond in a medium-sized but shallow cave, by means of a door casting. Commander Jaykarn, leader of the mercenaries working for the sorceress, shook his head as the sorceress stood back.

'How is that meant to keep them in?' he asked. 'It's just a shadow.'

Yolantha rapped a knuckle against it. The sound was dull and flat, like solid rock. Jaykarn ran a finger down the wall of blackness. It felt like warm glass.

'Very good, Ladyship. Now there is another matter to discuss.'

'As if I could not guess. Money?'

'Money. Your venture has failed, and there are roughly two thousand warriors, artisans and carters who are owed silver, a total of four hundred thousand silver shillings.'

'I have the money from Griffid's hoard. It is back at Highport, safely banked.'

'If you have no further use for us, we need to be paid and sent on our way. I suggest that you travel back to Highport and release the money to me.'

'I cannot travel, I was greatly weakened by attempting to build the portal tower. I shall scribe out a note of release to you. Collect the silver and fetch it back here.'

'You trust me with four hundred thousand silver shillings?'

'No, I trust that every mercenary on the continent will be after your blood if you run off. Now go.'

Two days weren't really enough time for Elvar to recover, but she decided to leave anyway. She kept her goodbyes brief, and gave the crowds that had gathered the excuse that what she needed to do next might save the world. She could still hear the cheers from the city when she was in the air and two miles away.

'I was very impressed with the way you behaved in Havenport,' Elvar told Winston. She had reached her preferred height and found a thermal to glide in. 'Anyone else would have stayed there and enjoyed the adoration.'

Lucky I'm not anyone else! You ate rats and mice to shut down my thoughts!

'Now don't go all whimpering servant boy on me, Winston. It doesn't suit you.'

Winston maintained silence for a moment. Then, *What are your plans for when we return?*

'Get the Imperium Key back from Yolantha.'

How?

'You don't need to know.'

Which means your plan is stupid and dangerous, there's a high probability of failure, and you're too embarrassed to talk about what you want to do.

'That more or less describes it. Is there anything you would like to do first? Maybe wash down our repast with some fine mulled wine?'

Very funny. Just warn any wizards left at the sanctum to pack everything they can carry, and run. Griffid is sure to call past eventually.

'You do not ask for much.'

I've never had much, so I'm good at doing without. What do you want?

'A body. I'm marooned on this world, and I would like independence from you – no offence, of course.'

None taken – the feeling's mutual. If anything can be done, I'll do it.

Chapter Ten

The trip home was filled with problems that neither Winston nor Elvar could have anticipated. A mapmaker had translated miles wrongly from a unit of distance double that of standard Dravinian miles. This transformed an ocean from a two-thousand-mile inconvenience to be crossed in twenty-four hours, into a four-thousand-mile chasm. Elvar was forced to land on a reef that was only above water at low tide, then fight off crabs the size of wolf hounds. The crabs turned out to be very good eating, however.

The cave where Faramond and Larissa were being kept was a natural formation, but the door wasn't. Faramond didn't like the darkness, so he conjured a tiny pinpoint of light that floated just below the ceiling. Each day Yolantha would dissolve the door and enter to question them about how the dragon portal was destroyed, but there wasn't much to be learned. Winston and Elvar had told Larissa very little, so that neither torture nor truth spells could extract any secrets from her. Faramond knew nothing, of course.

To say that Larissa and Faramond didn't get along would be an understatement. Faramond was constantly arguing that he was bigger than her, and needed more than half of the daily ration of food that Yolantha brought with her. Larissa told him that he could try living off the very ample padding around his stomach. On the first day of the third week of their captivity, the tension between them finally boiled over. Larissa had been dozing, but although Faramond moved very stealthily for someone of his size, the slightest rustle of cloth seemed quite loud in the confines of the cave. Larissa opened her eyes in time to see a podgy hand reaching out for the bag of trail biscuits and cheese that was meant to be her ration for the day. Faramond was too focused on the food to notice her watching.

The heel of the human foot delivers the strongest blow of any part of the body, because the leg is long and muscular, and the heel is backed up by a lot of bone. Using her leg like a club, Larissa chopped down on Faramond's hand. He shrieked with pain as bones, ligaments and nerves were severely stressed. The wizard now made a mistake that was all too common among men in Larissa's past. He assumed that she was weaker than him. Faramond was indeed strong, but only about evenly matched with Larissa.

At first, he tried to simply push her aside. She pushed back. Neither of them got anywhere. He then tried to wrestle with her. Faramond didn't know how to wrestle. Larissa did. After a few frantic moments of struggle, Larissa climbed astride the wizard, reached around his head and grabbed two handfuls of his beard. These she used like the reins of a horse. Like a horse, Faramond tried to buck her off. Larissa had learned that one stayed on a bucking horse by digging in with one's heels.

Unfortunately, she allowed herself to enjoy the ride. Worse, she forgot that the cave's roof was lower at the sides, and failed to notice that Faramond was bucking and heaving in that direction. A flash of light like a brilliant blue star blazed out before her eyes.

Larissa awoke to see Faramond munching down the last of her trail biscuits. She put a hand to her head and groaned.

'You have just learned a valuable lesson in life, you wretched girl,' said Faramond, having swallowed the last mouthful of biscuits and taken out the cheese. 'Never come between a Countercast wizard and his food.'

'My rations . . .'

'Ah, but possession is nine-tenths of the law, and I have possession.'

'Yolantha will punish . . .' began Larissa, then the cave swam before her eyes.

'Yolantha hates you even more than she does me. It's eat quickly or go hungry in here.'

It was Faramond's smugness that was his downfall, because it annoyed Larissa more intensely than a hungry flea under plate armour. She launched herself across at him, and a moment later was astride his back again. This time she drove her heel into a very special point just above his right knee, where a nerve isn't very well protected by muscle. Faramond screamed with pain, and his leg collapsed. Larissa grabbed his right arm and twisted it behind his back. She grasped his index finger and snapped it.

'This little piggy went to market!' she said above Faramond's screams.

She grasped his middle finger.

'This little piggy stayed at home!' *Snap!*

The shadow door collapsed at that very moment.

Yolantha had watched as Griffid flamed her entire encampment. He had blasted her with such intense flame that the rocks beneath her feet glowed red. He hadn't looked back after swooping over her, however, and so didn't notice that she was still standing and unharmed. The Imperium Key hung around her neck, even protecting her from dragon fire.

As Griffid did a wide, leisurely circle of the encampment to check whether he had missed anything, Yolantha crouched out of sight. Finally, he flew off, heading east. The sorceress hurried up to the cave's entrance, traced an unlocking spell, and pressed it against the shadow door. It dissolved. Yolantha's eyes widened. Larissa was astride Faramond, blood streaming down her face and one of Faramond's unbroken fingers in her hand. In Faramond's left hand was a cut of cheese.

'I can explain,' said Larissa and Faramond together.

'I won't even ask,' said the sorceress. She gestured out over a landscape of charred bodies and burning wagons, tents and stores.

'The Imperium Key that I wear protected me from even Griffid's deadly flames, so bear that in mind before you try to attack me, warrior girl. Now come along, both of you.'

There was no shortage of roasted horse flesh lying about, so they soon had enough meat for several days – cut into slices and stuffed into improvised backpacks – as well as some slightly scorched trail biscuits that had survived Griffid's fire.

'There is one relatively undamaged wagon,' said Yolantha, once they were ready to leave. 'Faramond, do that chicken leg casting on the wagon, and take us to Highport.'

'Only Winston knows that one, Ladyship.

Besides, this evil wench broke the finger that I use to trace spells.'

'He was stealing my rations!' exclaimed Larissa.

'Enough!' shouted Yolantha. 'We walk to Highport. Come along.'

'But Ladyship, my feet—' began Faramond.

'A word of warning, Faramond,' said Yolantha. 'One more word about your feet and Larissa will ride on your shoulders, all the way back to Highport. She seems quite adept at that. And try to sneak one single mouthful of meat without my permission, and I shall ration you to one dragon-charred trail biscuit per day!'

As luck would have it, they hadn't travelled half a mile before they met with the commander of the mercenaries, returning from Highport with his personal guardsmen, and leading pack donkeys loaded with silver shillings. They were on a stone arch bridge that spanned a narrow chasm through which the Harst River flowed. Yolantha, backed up by her two prisoners, confronted Commander Jaykarn, his two contract wizards and the twenty riders of his escort.

'There are two thousand folk who won't want paying,' said Yolantha, with a casual wave at the smoking, blackened scene behind her. 'Two hundred silver shillings for one officer, same each contract wizards, and twenty horsemen of the escort at a hundred silver shillings each. You may take two thousand-six-hundred silver shillings and go. The rest goes to Highport with me.'

Commander Jaykarn leaned forward in his saddle and drew his sword.

'Ladyship, might I respectfully point out that you command only a girl and a very poor excuse for a wizard. I have twenty mercenary cavalry and two wizards to back me up. In the light of your changed circumstances, I am inclined to keep all four-hundred-thousand shillings.'

Yolantha's eyebrow rose. 'But I have a dragon.'

'I see no dragon,' said Jaykarn, glancing up at the sky.

Yolantha traced the spell for dragon in the air, where it hung, glowing.

'That will summon any dragon within a hundred miles,' said one of the wizards behind

Jaykarn, 'and by the look of this place there is definitely a dragon within that distance.'

'If the dragon returned, you would die, too,' said Jaykarn, laughing.

Some of the men behind him joined in his laughter, although a little more nervously.

'Dragons can't kill me, as you can see,' said Yolantha, 'but all of you can be roasted alive.'

'You were hiding in that cave with the two prisoners.'

'I was facing down the dragon, and he couldn't kill me. Shall we do a little test? Dismount, and let us trade blows with our swords. First, you cut at my neck, then I cut at yours.'

Jaykarn cautiously dismounted. Yolantha was too confident. He hefted his sword. Yolantha sheathed her sword and folded her arms, then nodded at him. He swung his blade in a flat arc. The blade shattered like glass when it struck Yolantha's neck. Jaykarn backed away.

'I could demand the right to strike once at your neck, Commander Jaykarn, but I only wanted to show that I am invulnerable. Shall I clap over the spell that hangs in the air and speak the name of the dragon? Answer carefully.'

Jaykarn glanced back at his men. They shifted uneasily.

'I think we can come to an arrangement,' he said.

'You will be paid what we agreed originally, and I will keep the rest.'

'Agreed.'

'I want a horse, so two of your men must share a horse. The silver from two of the donkeys will be carried by some of your men, so that the warrior girl and Faramond can ride . . .' She broke off, then screeched, 'Faramond!'

The wizard had absently unstrapped his makeshift pack and taken out a slice of dragon-roasted horseflesh, which he was now devouring. On Yolantha's order, Faramond was seized.

'What did I say about eating without permission?' she asked.

'But Ladyship, the trip to Highport will only be a few days, now that we have horses.'

'Who said anything about you riding, Faramond? You're going to walk, but your ration of meat is going to fly.'

Yolantha picked up Faramond's pack, walked over to the edge of the bridge, and dropped it into the raging waters far below.

'No!' he screamed, but his rations were beyond rescue.

'Faramond, I'm going to give you a choice,' Yolantha continued. 'You may walk and have ten trail biscuits per day, or you may ride a donkey and have one biscuit. If you walk, we shall not ride slowly so that you can keep up. Two of your fingers are broken, so you cannot trace defensive spells. These mountains are full of bears, wolves and any number of other things with a taste for well-fed wizards.'

'I'll ride, and make do with one biscuit,' muttered Faramond.

Before long the small convoy of riders was heading back to Highport. Yolantha rode beside Faramond, holding a tether that was tied around his neck.

'Commander Jaykarn was right, you're a very poor excuse for a wizard,' said Yolantha. 'I keep you alive because you're useful. Cease to be useful and I shall abandon you to starve or be eaten.'

'Understood, Ladyship.'

'Griffid returned, so he obviously never left this world. What does that mean?'

'It means that dragons are native to this world,' replied Faramond, concentrating as if his life hung in the balance – which it did. 'They didn't come through some portal opened by a foolish wizard.'

'Perfectly correct. My portal must have opened on the other side of our world. However, just before the portal collapsed, an iffryt was seen plunging into it. That means there is at least one iffryt left in this world, and I can use that iffryt to build another portal. A proper portal, to the iffryt world which is overcharged with power. I shall heal your broken fingers and let you live, but you are going to help me.'

'Help you by becoming part of a living portal to another world for thousands of years?'

'Look upon it as easy work, ideal for a lazy wizard.'

Three weeks to the day after plunging into the portal, Winston and Elvar soared over the Dravinian coast, a hundred miles north of Haldan.

Yolantha's sanctum is another sixty miles to the west,

said Winston, trying to imagine the landscape far below him as a huge map.

'Is that a good place to start?' asked Elvar.

No place is a good place to start, but that one is closest.

'I am fresh enough to get there.'

Two hours later they were circling the charred, blackened remains of Yolantha's palace of power. Nothing capable of burning remained unburned, including the once impressive door of eyes.

Griffid's already back! said Winston once they had landed. *Look at the claw marks on that wall.*

'Are those skeletons?' asked Elvar.

Those are scattered human bones, said Winston. *Probably one of Yolantha's wizards. Are the stones warm?*

'No more so than the surrounding desert.'

Then Griffid is long gone.

At that moment they heard a scrabbling nearby.

'Humans?' cried a slurred voice.

'Small dragon!' Elvar called back.

'Please, come in. Dragons . . . welcome. I like dragons. A dragon made me master of the Countercasts' Guild Sanctum.'

A wizard in grubby, ragged robes staggered into view.

Guild Inquisitor, prompted Winston in Elvar's mind.

'You're the Guild Inquisitor, aren't you?' said Elvar.

'Guild Master now, gracious thanks to . . . dragon. Killed everyone else.'

'What happened here? I mean, when the other dragon arrived?'

'Not sure. I was in the wine cellar, everyone else was at dinner.'

'They must have seen the dragon coming.'

'Yes, but . . . you know how wizards are. Wouldn't interrupt a good meal for . . . end of the world.'

'Were the Lady Yolantha and the hermit wizard Faramond here?'

'No, she had sent a message . . . by bird. Join her at Blackstone Tower, she said. Only six of us stayed to mind the place.'

'And you were in the wine cellar.'

'Lucky, that. Sounded too dangerous outside, so I drank a few bottles to pass the time. Thought

I was to die, so I took off my robes and marinated myself in a vat of Dalaran spring vintage. Thought the dragon might appreciate that, but . . . it flew off. It's been wine or nothing since then. All that's to be eaten was torched, along with everything else.'

'So Yolantha and Faramond are still alive?'

'I care not,' the wizard said.

Far away in Harst Mountains, another wizard was resorting to extreme measures to escape Yolantha without getting himself killed. One day's travel from Highport, Faramond stole some food, knowing that there was an alarm spell on it, and that he would get caught at once. Yolantha now sentenced him to half a biscuit per day, and having to walk instead of riding.

Yolantha's mistake was thinking that Faramond was stupid and lazy. He was definitely lazy, yet passably intelligent and brilliantly cunning. Using his last reserves of fat, he cast a spell on one of the donkeys to look like himself. The donkey tether around his neck was not at all magical, it was only to humiliate him. He quickly untied it and tossed it into a roadside chasm. Yolantha had enchanted the food packs with alarm spells, yet she hadn't done so with the silver. After all, what was there to spend it on out there?

Faramond helped himself to a half dozen silver coins, not enough to be noticed until the whole lot was counted. An hour before dawn he slipped away, then did what nobody could ever have expected him to do. Because he was now quite thin, he was able to run, or at least manage a brisk jog. The faint half-light was enough to show him the trail, and by mid-morning he shuffled into Highport on bleeding feet. He bought himself six freshly baked pies, three roast chickens and a flagon of ale, then paid a wharfman to put him in a large sack and carry him onto a barge that was about to leave for the trip down the river.

At first, Yolantha's men thought one of the donkeys had escaped, and wasted an hour searching for it. Faramond seemed to be still there. They then loaded the remaining donkeys. Yolantha told them to make Faramond carry some of the missing donkey's load, but although the image of Faramond stood before them, when they tried to strap a pack onto him, what they felt was a donkey. The enraged Yolantha broke the spell in a moment, but then made the mistake of assuming that Faramond was too lazy to flee and was hiding nearby, waiting for them to move on. Another two hours were lost while they searched for him. When Yolantha finally reached Highport, she asked if a fat man in ragged wizard's clothing had been seen boarding a barge or buying a horse that day. When told that no fat, ragged wizard had done any such thing that day, she concluded that Faramond was now hiding in Highport, and announced a large reward for any information about him.

The following day, Faramond abandoned the barge at Earthshift, bought himself a knife, a blanket and a large meal, then set off for the ruins of Kalderial. Until now he was feeling pleased with himself for escaping Yolantha, but that didn't last. Even with his fingers healed and his ability to trace spells restored, he remained a hopeless hunter. Although Kalderial's ruins contained a lot of game, catching it was much harder than he had ever imagined, and after just a few days, he was getting seriously tired of foraging for wild fruit and vegetables.

'First, catch your boar,' muttered Faramond, tracing a spell to attract any boar that was within a hundred yards. 'How hard can that be?'

The wizard grasped the sharpened branch that was meant to be his boar spear and waited. A boar trotted out of the nearby bushes, and immediately saw that Faramond was not a fellow creature. It charged. The wizard panicked, dropped his improvised boar spear and – with astonishing luck for someone so unlucky – leapt straight up and grasped the branch above him. The branch broke. There was a muffled but distinct snap as Faramond landed on the boar, breaking its neck.

'Well, I'll be.' Faramond sat breathless for a moment. 'Sometimes, just sometimes, I really miss having Winston around the place,' he mused, patting the boar's carcass.

Elvar and Winston stayed the night at the ruins of the Countercasts' Sanctum, and before the inquisitor was awake, Elvar flew off for Haldan. Here they decided to take a chance that their shared body was well enough nourished to endure another morphing, so Winston could resume his natural shape. Nobody in the port city had heard from Yolantha or Faramond. Winston retrieved Larissa's horse from Stylan.

So, we go on to Kalderial? asked Elvar as Winston rode for the city gates.

'For Faramond, it's home. If he's alive and free, he'll be there.'

It took the rest of the day to reach the ruins of Kalderial. After a year and a half of tracking boars through the ancient city, Winston had no trouble picking up signs of Faramond. The wizard had installed himself in the ruins of a mansion that had once belonged to one of the city's royal courtiers.

'Master, I know you're in there!' Winston shouted.

'Winston?' called Faramond from the tangle of greenery ahead.

'Winston Spellwyn, aye,' he called back.

Faramond pushed aside a curtain of vines and ivy, looked around suspiciously, and finally emerged. While still not at all thin, Winston estimated that he now weighed no more than two hundred pounds.

'Is this your new home, Master?' asked Winston.

'Home? Home? Idiot boy, I have no home. That damnable dragon arrived here and set the entire palace on fire. Fortunately, I was away from my hut, answering a call of nature.'

'How very lucky, Master.'

'How did you ever manage to catch so much game in this place?' Faramond babbled softly. 'Even with entrapment snares I can scarcely catch enough to keep body and spirit together. Butchering them for the fire is quite the most disgusting task imaginable.'

'Master, I need to know the fate of two people,' said Winston, ignoring Faramond's query. 'One of them is a girl named Larissa.'

'The wench who wears armour and pretends to be a knight? Yolantha has her.'

'She's alive?' gasped Winston.

'Last I saw of her, yes.'

'Praise to the gods,' Winston whispered. 'The

other is Yolantha herself.'

'What? Yolantha? You didn't lead her here did you, stupid boy?'

'No, Master.'

'That wretched woman tried to turn Griffid into a new portal tower on Blackstone Mountain, but it collapsed and Griffid vanished. Yolantha was furious. There was great confusion after the tower collapsed and disappeared, so I was able to escape.'

'What of Larissa?' Winston insisted, suddenly full of hope. 'Is she injured? Tell me of her!'

'The last time I saw her she was bruised and bleeding, but alive. She killed a guard and a wizard, and disrupted whatever Lady Yolantha was doing with the new portal tower.'

'Where's the sorceress now?'

'Highport, I think.'

'Highport? Not Blackstone?'

'She was going to Highport when I escaped.'

'Thank you. Now I should go, Master. Is there anything you need?'

'Yes! A new and obedient apprentice who has some respect for me! I'm too frightened to stay in any place for more than a day in case Griffid finds me – or Yolantha, I don't know which would be worse. Whoever heard of a nomad hermit?'

Winston no longer looked like a Provisional Wizard when he set off for Earthshift. He was dressed like a journeyman artisan and was riding a horse, and he even had some silver, courtesy of some dead slave merchant on the other side of the world.

'I wonder if we can trust Faramond,' he said. 'Yolantha may have let him go so he could lie to us.'

Tell me, Winston, how many roads are there past Highport? asked Elvar in his mind.

'Just the one. We passed along it, remember? You were shaped like a giant cat. It caused a great deal of alarm.'

And Highport is the closest city to Blackstone Mountain?

Winston shrugged. 'Of course.'

Would you say that Yolantha enjoys her luxuries?

'Yes, I suppose so.'

If she were waiting for us to come looking for Larissa, do you think she would stay in a tent at Blackstone

Mountain, or in a city that we have to pass through to get there?

Winston pondered her words, but not for long. 'You're building a strong case for Highport.'

Highport is a hundred and sixty miles from here, most of that by barge. Can you imagine Faramond escaping Yolantha and fleeing four hundred miles back to Kalderial all by himself?

'Perhaps not.'

Whether or not Faramond is spreading lies for her, I think Yolantha is waiting in comfort at Highport, holding Larissa hostage, and preparing to ambush us.

'How could she possibly know that we survived?'

Griffid paid the Countercasts' Guild Sanctuary a visit and burned it. If Griffid can return, then so could we.

'Do you have a plan?'

We go to Highport and get ambushed.

Winston frowned. 'Then?'

It's like with the tower.

'Ah, so we cross my fingers and hope for the best.'

I know how Yolantha thinks, Winston. I served her for a long time.

'And that's it? You think you know what she might do?'

Three quarters of winning a battle is knowing how the enemy commander thinks.

'And the other quarter is having an army. We don't have one. Yolantha does.'

Well, what would you do?

'Go to Highport.'

Ah, splendid.

'By barge. The horse stays in the public stables at Earthshift.'

Why? A barge going upstream is three times slower than a rider.

'Because I've grown rather fond of him, and Valiant would get shot from under us if we got ambushed.'

Valiant?

'That's his name.'

Larissa never told you his name. I would have noticed.

'I've decided that he's Valiant. It's the sort of silly name she would have given him.'

The barge takes five days. Why bother?

'Ah, but Haldan is just one day away because it's downstream and the barge moves three times faster. From there it's half a day's ride to Loseros.'

Haldan? Loseros? exclaimed Elvar. *What about Highport? You're losing me.*

'Then we take another barge all the way upstream to Highport.'

You have lost me.

'Elvar, I'm going to my home village to raise an army.'

What? How big is your home village?

'Five hundred souls, maybe.'

Last I saw, Yolantha had more than twice as many experienced warriors in her pay.

'But my warriors are better. I shall recruit my mother, grandmother, sister Porrel and her dog Fang. If Stanni's ship is in port we might get her, too.'

Those are odds of two hundred to one.

'Not counting Fang.'

You are either barking mad, or you have a very, very cunning plan.

'Yes, I have a plan, and it's indeed cunning.'

What is it?

'I can't tell you.'

Why not – and don't say you just like surprises.

'Elvar, when I explain my scheme to defeat Yolantha to my family, it'll become obvious why I'm not telling you just now. Relax, enjoy the journey. After a few days on the barges, I'll be better rested if we have to transform into you.'

A week went by. Winston travelled to Haldan, then Loseros. He then returned to Haldan, and bought passage on a barge bound for Highport. The river sailor collecting fares stared at Winston carefully, checked his face against a sketch, then waved him past. This was in spite of the fact that the sketch was a very good likeness of Winston.

Now I understand why you did not explain your plan to me on the way to your home village, said Elvar in Winston's mind.

'Yes,' said Winston softly, after glancing about to make sure nobody was within earshot. 'You would've spent the entire trip to Loseros telling me that it's insanely dangerous, and that I should think of something else.'

But it is insanely dangerous.

'And I cannot think of anything else.'

If I pester you all the way to Highport, will you abandon this plan and try to think of something else?

'No.'

I'm beginning to see why Faramond gets along so badly with you.

The trip on the barge was quite uneventful. One of the other passengers was a garbage collector, travelling to Highport to better himself, and everyone else was astounded that Winston was willing to endure the smell and talk to him.

Winston's story was that he was a metalsmith's apprentice, travelling to meet with his master in Highport. It was on the evening of the tenth day that the barge tied up at the Highport docks. The local magistrate's militiamen boarded immediately, and each of them was holding a parchment sketch of a face.

'Oi, found him!' shouted the first man to catch sight of Winston.

'But I'm not lost!' Winston said, feigning ignorance of his position.

Flee! Elvar screamed.

'To where?' he said as he was surrounded by

men with drawn sabres, while others cocked crossbows or unslung ropes.

'Shut him up!' someone commanded.

'Bind his hands first, he's a wizard,' ordered the sergeant of the squad. 'Don't let him trace a spell, there's no telling what he might do.'

Winston was quickly gagged and bound so thoroughly that he was unable to walk, so the militiamen carried him off the barge. A cart was waiting on the pier, and it was in this that he was driven to the magistrate's hall. Here he was exchanged for a large bag of silver. After an hour a covered wagon was driven to the back entrance, and Winston was exchanged for an even larger bag of silver. The wagon hadn't gone far when the wagon that was supposed to collect Winston from the magistrate's hall caught up. There was a brief but bloody battle as those working for Yolantha persuaded the one of Highport's local gangs to hand him over.

Winston had been gagged and so thoroughly wrapped in ropes that very little of his clothing was visible, but he hadn't been blindfolded. Thus, he saw the sign of the Waterfall's Rest tavern as he was carried inside. Winston was tied to a chair, then Yolantha swept into the room. She was dressed as a cavalryman in riding trousers and a blue jacket, but no cavalryman on the continent had a jacket of padded silk with buttons made of gold. Yolantha removed Winston's gag but left the rest of him bound. She stood back, seemingly relishing this moment.

'So nice to feel wanted,' said Winston.

Yolantha laughed. 'Boy, I made sure you are wanted by everyone on the roads from Haldan, Kalderial, and what is left of Loseros.'

'I came by barge.'

'The barge crews also had copies of your sketch. I'm surprised none of the crew recognised you.'

'Can't get reliable help these days,' said Winston.

'Actually, the captain did recognise you and deliberately let you sail with him. But I can't get reliable wizards.' She tilted her head. 'Is this how you repay me after I granted you your certificate?'

'Provisional status. Besides, you were doing things that were bad for everyone else, and everyone else included me.'

'Pah,' she scoffed. 'I was doing what is best

for everyone. Too many fools are in positions of power.'

'Why bother with me? I'm not powerful.'

'Winston, on the way here from Blackstone Mountain, I had a long talk with Faramond. He was very willing to talk in exchange for an occasional trail biscuit. He told me that you were brave enough to liberate Elvar from her phial. Amazingly, she didn't tear you to pieces, but became your travelling companion.'

'We did seem to get on.'

'Are you aware that Faramond borrowed your farsight tube when you and Elvar climbed Blackstone Mountain to the original tower?'

'Didn't he say he was with me?'

'You mean didn't he lie that he was with you. He said that he saw a single creature fly out of the collapsing tower. You can't fly, Elvar can. He watched it land at the base of the mountain, then watched as it walked back to where he was lying with his feet in the air. Imagine his surprise when it turned out to be you.'

'I prefer the story where he climbed the mountain with me and hit me over the head.'

'But I don't. When I was building my tower

out of Griffid, I was too busy stopping the idiot warrior girl when she attacked. But some of my mercenaries said they saw a flying creature circle it, then somehow evade my ward spells and plunge into the portal before its form was properly locked in place. The accounts of armed peasants are not known to be reliable, but those who saw the thing all described it as a giant bat. Bats don't look like dragons, not even baby dragons. They look like iffryts.'

'All iffryts escaped back to their own world before the first portal was closed and sealed.'

'Most did,' agreed Yolantha, waving a finger and smirking. 'The iffryt that I merged with three thousand years ago abandoned me as well.'

'You? You were part iffryt?'

'I was, and I gained quite a taste for immortality. Now he has gone. But from what Faramond says, Elvar is still in this world and merged with you. I want her back.' Yolantha's black eyes glared.

'She's a person,' Winston said, 'and not to be traded like some horse.'

'I could threaten to kill you. I might even do it.'

'But that will kill Elvar as well. Immortality and invulnerability aren't the same thing.'

'I know you have a fondness for her.'

'I do,' Winston agreed. 'That's why I won't give her up.'

'How do you feel about Lady Larissa de Green?' she asked.

Winston glared at Yolantha but didn't reply.

'Ah, do I detect a love triangle?'

'Larissa is dead. One doesn't go against odds of a thousand to one and survive.'

'She sustained injuries, but five weeks of restful captivity have healed the worst of them. Make a choice, Winston. Immortality in a body shared with an iffryt, or mortality with a nobleman's daughter in a separate body. She is in distress, and you are honourable.'

'I don't even know that she's alive.'

'Oh, I can prove that easily enough. I'm going to free your legs, then take you for a ride in a very fine carriage that I bought out of what remains of Griffid's hoard.'

Elvar was strangely silent.

Yolantha led a blindfolded Winston down to the carriage. Although the ride was no more than a mile, the streets of the inland port soon came to sound like the rough and dangerous maze where Winston had grown up. The blindfold was not removed until they were in what looked like the office of a warehouse. Predictably there were at least two dozen more men present, playing cards and having their evening meal. One was wearing a full suit of plate armour and chainmail, and at a gesture from Yolantha he picked up his helmet and a dish of something brown with a spoon in it. Yolantha and Winston stopped at a window set into a wall. The man in armour walked on.

Winston looked through greenish glass which was at least half an inch thick. He froze. On the other side, in the middle of the room, was Larissa. She was still in the same clothes she had been wearing when Winston had last seen her, five weeks earlier. A lantern on a peg illuminated the scene. She was in a mesh cage with a bucket, and surrounding the cage was a carpet of rats.

The man in armour entered the room, now wearing his helmet and carrying the bowl of what appeared to be a meal for the captive girl. The rats were obviously starving, because they attacked the armoured man's chainmail leggings and boots. He opened a slot high in the side of the cage and passed the bowl through to Larissa. She immediately flung the contents through the mesh at him, which caused the frantic rats to swarm up his chainmail to get at the food that was now smeared over him. He lumbered out, beating at the layer of rats that was swarming over him.

'A few rats escape when the door opens and closes, but I make sure that an extra barrel of the rodents is added each day,' said Yolantha.

'Larissa!' shouted Winston, but she didn't turn toward the window.

'She can't hear you,' said Yolantha. 'The glass is thick and the rats make a lot of noise. She has been trying to starve herself since we arrived here.'

Winston was too transfixed to pay much attention to Yolantha.

'She must know that you're using her as ransom to force me to betray Elvar,' Winston said, still distracted.

'We clear out the rats and force-feed her every week. Seen enough?'

'I want to see her set free.'

'Oh, I can arrange that. In fact, we are returning to the Waterfall's Rest now. Bind Elvar to me, and I shall have Lady Larissa brought there unharmed, bathed, clothed in robes from the finest tailor on Waterview Street, then left with your gallant self and a sumptuous meal for both of you. Think quickly, however. Unless I have your cooperation within the hour, the cage will be raised. The men here are really sick of looking after her.'

Yolantha inverted an hourglass, and then blindfolded Winston again. Winston sat sullenly silent in the carriage all the way back to the tavern. Once alone in her suite of rooms, she removed the blindfold and freed his hands. She didn't seem in a hurry.

'What I want is very simple, Winston. I want you to grant me the iffryt Elvar,' she said as he rubbed the circulation back into his fingers. 'Do nothing foolish. I have some quite lethal spells prepared and just a snap of my fingers will set them onto you.'

'Elvar is my friend, I can't just give her away.'

'Then the rats are in for a treat tonight.'

'You don't understand. I can't give her to you because I can't trust you.'

'Just as I don't trust you.'

And just for the record, I don't trust your plan, said Elvar in Winston's mind.

'Then how do we solve this?'

'Think of something. I'm very patient.'

'You could release Larissa and put me in the cage.'

'Not a wise choice for me. You are the heroic type. Heroes are more likely to make sacrifices for others than for themselves.'

She certainly has your measure, said Elvar.

'Then what am I to do?' Winston asked Yolantha.

'I want the iffryt. Sell her to me for the smallest copper coin in circulation in this kingdom. By the rules of magical service, that will bind her.'

She held up a coin, which was not big enough to cover a fingernail.

'Will you cast Iffryt Elvar's services to me?'

'Yes – but I want her safe.'

'Oh, no. Safe means the pressure is eased upon you.'

Yolantha traced a spell in the air, then spoke Larissa's name. A pale image of Larissa materialised amid a writhing swarm of rat fangs and claws. They attacked the image of Larissa, stripping her down to a skeleton as she tried to fight back, then dispersed like glowing smoke.

'What you have just seen was a promise, not a threat,' said Yolantha. 'Now trace the spell and speak the words.'

Winston let his shoulders sag, as if accepting defeat.

'Iffryt Elvar, I hereby transfer all the bindings and obligations between myself and yourself to the Sorceress Yolantha, on the condition that she releases me and frees Lady Larissa de Green.'

'Clever,' said Yolantha as she unbuttoned her jacket.

The Imperium Key was hanging from her neck. She grasped it with her left hand, then held out her right with the coin on her palm.

'Hold hands and accept your payment, Winston.'

Winston reached out to her. There was a bright flash, and pain as intense as that from picking up a red-hot poker as the coin touched his skin. All at once, silvery tendrils materialised and bound their hands together.

'Oh, and one small detail,' said Yolantha. 'You will need to go to the storehouse. Do you think you can find it within what is left of the hour?'

'I don't have to. Do your worst, Elvar.'

With the greatest of pleasure.

Yolantha let out a scream, wrenching at her hand. It remained bound to Winston's. She tried to let go of the Imperium Key, but her left hand was no longer under her control. Winston felt something like rushing water throughout his body, except it was beneath his skin. He saw Yolantha's body blur for a moment, and she swayed on her feet as if about to faint. Winston released her hand and helped her to a chair, then went across to a window and threw the shutters open.

'It's done, Grandmother!' he shouted into the night.

Down in the street, an old woman with shark teeth and a horsehair wig steadied herself, carefully leaning a crutch against a wall, then made a gesture of release for a spell that had been set up but not yet cast. She snapped her fingers.

All over the waterfront area of Highport, everyone who had eaten at any one of the dozens of pie carts, taverns, street-side cafes and bakeries suddenly doubled over with cramps and made for whatever resembled a toilet that was nearby. Most didn't make it. Outside a particular warehouse, a man with a definite smell of garbage about him picked up a small dog with a very eager attitude where rats were concerned. The river sailor standing with him took a hatchet from under his jacket and got to work on the door of the warehouse office. Once inside, those who were meant to be guarding Larissa de Green didn't trouble them. After a minute or so of searching, the man with the rank odour unbolted a thick, stout door, pulled it open, tossed his dog inside and called, 'Get 'em, Fang.'

The rats might have been starving, but they weren't stupid. Faced with a dog that was going to take no nonsense from any rat and an open door, the vast majority chose the door. Someone unfamiliar to Larissa now entered the room. He smelled of rotting vegetables and fish. At that moment the cage was drawn upwards by the chain from the hole in the roof.

'Oi, warrior girl, we're from Winston and we're here to help,' said the youth, reaching out to her. 'Come along, the barge is waiting.'

'Are you unhurt?' asked a sailor who joined them outside.

'Not been eating,' she mumbled. 'Long time.'

'Best you carry her,' commanded Fang's owner.

Chapter Eleven

Within minutes they were on a barge tied up at the docks. Not one of the clerks, labourers, carters or merchants was in any state to stop them. In fact, most were crouched on the edge of the pier with their trousers down. As the sailor carried her down the loading plank, Larissa thought she recognised the two women who were already aboard. The sailor laid her on a pile of sacks beside them, then cast off the moorings and pushed at the pier with a bargepole. The current drew the barge away.

'Best you have a little bread and ale first,' said the elder of the two women.

'I know you,' said Larissa weakly. 'It's Gran Spellwyn and Mother Spellwyn.'

'Aye, it's us, and ye might remember our girl Porrel collectin' the garbage.' Larissa realised that the youth with the rank body odour and the dog was a girl. 'Stanni, now she knows boats like I know herbs.'

The sailor with the barge pole waved to Larissa.

'And I know spells for bowel cramps,' added Winston's grandmother.

'What just happened?' Larissa asked.

'Oh, Winston collected us from Loseros before coming here. Hired a wagon to take us to Haldan. Very fancy, it was.'

'I meant what just happened back in Highport?'

'After Winston were taken off the barge, Fang trailed him. He's clever like that. Meantime we asked a few questions and learned that a hoity lady was buyin' rats at ten times the goin' rate. Gran also spread a nasty little spell over just about every eatery within a mile of the docks.'

'Fair walked me feet off, took most of the day,' said Gran Spellwyn.

'While we did that, Stanni got to talkin' to some workers in a tavern and learned about a lady wantin' a rat-proof cage built in a hurry, couple of weeks back.'

'Fang showed me the Waterfall's Rest, and the warehouse where Winston were took,' called Porrel from downwind.

Larissa put her hands to her head. 'I'm still not sure what happened.'

'Winston reckoned he had a way to get some key back from the lady what were holdin' you,' said Mother Spellwyn. 'Nasty type, she was. Once it were done, he signalled Gran and she set things in motion.'

'Bowels, mainly,' added Gran.

'Wait a moment!' said Larissa. 'You mean Winston got the Imperium Key back from Lady Yolantha?'

'Reckon so.'

'Then . . . all is good.'

'That it is.'

'I think I'll have a rest now.'

'Not until you've had some bread and ale. Don't worry, the food we left on the barge wasn't under that spell.'

Larissa managed a smile. 'And thank you for rescuing me.'

'Why, think nothin' of it, luv. You used to be such a cutie, on the pony with your parchment armour and curtain rod.'

Back in Highport, in the Waterfall's Rest, Elvar was in Yolantha's body, locked in the privy. Yolantha had eaten local food within the past twelve hours, and her body was suffering the effects of Gran Spellwyn's spell.

'Nothing in this part of Highport will be safe to eat for another twelve hours,' called Winston.

'Go away!' Elvar called back with Yolantha's voice.

Winston picked up the Imperium Key and traced a spell. It was a very minor spell, but even so, he felt himself weaken slightly.

'How are you faring, Lady Yolantha?' he asked.

'You tricked me!' shrieked a tiny voice from the jewel inset in the key.

'I did exactly what you asked; I spoke the words and cast the spell transferring Elvar's bond to you. The problem was that we . . . were in a little trouble some months ago, and I had to let myself be bound to her or die. She was very nice about it.'

'You became a slave's slave?' squeaked Yolantha. 'I should have listened to Faramond. You are a filthy, despicable wretch!'

'Tut-tut, fair maiden.' Winston wagged a finger. 'You couldn't conceive of the idea that an iffryt held a bond upon me, a human wizard, and that I willingly let it happen. That was your weakness. When you tried to take control of her, you encountered a free iffryt. She no longer had the energies from the portal to her world, but her powers still outclassed yours. She bound you into the Imperium Key's jewel and took possession of your own body.'

'I hate you. I hate you both!'

'Temper! At least you're immortal again.'

'I'll destroy you! I'll destroy the world!'

'This is getting boring.' Winston traced a spell. 'Silence!' he said, flicking his fingers at the Imperium Key.

Yolantha's voice was cut off mid-shriek. Winston tossed her copper shot through the open window, then walked across to the privy door. He traced a spell, then clapped once. Elvar continued to groan.

Maybe that was the spell to cure piles, he thought, then traced another spell and clapped. The groans stopped.

'How are you faring?' he asked.

'Like a huge hand has stopped squeezing my intestines.'

'Well enough to ride?'

'If I have to.'

'Then we leave now and find a peasant willing to hide us in his hovel for a handful of silver shillings. This place is going to be full of very angry people asking awkward questions tomorrow.'

The following day, the barge reached Earthshift at sunset. Stanni tied up, then bought passage on another barge before the river port's clerk realised that Stanni's vessel had no papers and had probably been stolen. Larissa went to the stables and arranged for her horse to be put aboard the barge.

'What happens now?' asked Larissa as the second barge set off into the current, its side lamps lit and the crew pushing with their barge poles.

'You go home,' said Stanni.

'Not a good plan,' sighed Larissa.

'Father still angry?'

'Sure to be.'

'And your mother?'

Larissa made a face. 'Probably still screaming.'

'Your sister?'

'Very pleased, because father said he's written me out of his will.'

'Life's not kind to big, strong girls like us,' said Stanni, lying back and looking up at the stars. 'Do you know what was the happiest day of my life?'

Larissa tilted her head. 'Tell me.'

'I won an arm-wrestling match with my uncle. He said I was stronger than any of the sailors on his ship. I asked if he needed another sailor. He said yes.'

Larissa sighed. 'I was born into a rich family; strength is a big impediment for rich girls.'

'What do you really, really want to do, Ladyship? No knight will ever make you his squire, so a career in warfare is not in your future.'

'While I was with Winston, I discovered that I enjoyed travelling. If I had money, I'd set off to see the world.'

Stanni clasped Larissa by the shoulder. 'Work on a ship and you actually get paid to see the world.'

'Alas, I don't have an uncle who is captain of a ship.'

'But I can recommend you to *my* uncle.'

Some days later, Winston and Elvar arrived in the ruins of Kalderial. The mercenaries and wizards riding behind them only saw Lady Yolantha on a horse, holding a tether around Winston's neck. Winston was walking and wearing a heavy backpack. Around Elvar's neck was the chain holding the Imperium Key, in which Yolantha was trapped.

Elvar glanced back to make sure that none of the others were within earshot before speaking.

'Are you absolutely sure you want to do this?' she said softly.

'Absolutely sure,' Winston replied, without looking up.

'But as Yolantha, I have power and credibility. I plan to set up a new guild with those of the Countercasts' Guild who are still alive. You can be a founding elder.'

'At fourteen? That's not a very old elder. I know what's best for me.'

'Why return to Faramond? I can arrange for any of the finest wizards on the continent to teach you.'

'And I would respect them and do everything they tell me to. That's bad.'

'Bad? Talk sense.'

'Elvar, Faramond is lazy, greedy, incompetent and a bully. While with him, I was forced to become devious, and develop survival skills and magical strengths that no other apprentice has. I'm young, yet think of all I've managed to do. If I were apprenticed to a wise, kind wizard I would respect him and always do exactly what I was told. I'd never bother thinking for myself. I'd be just another apprentice, nothing special at all.'

'You can't know that.'

'Oh yes I can. I worked for my mother until I was twelve, and for all her faults, she's a fair, competent and hard-working herbalist. I was happy with her, but I never had a single original thought. With Faramond I was forced to think.'

'Your decision, Winston,' said Elvar, shaking Yolantha's head.

They entered the old palace, now free of trees,

bushes, vines and all other forms of vegetation. Griffid had called past and spewed fire on the place, just in case Faramond happened to be home. Now free of their covering of vegetation, the stone ruins of the ancient buildings gleamed a brilliant white in the sunlight, and could have been mistaken for a new palace that was being constructed.

'He's not moved back here,' said Elvar. 'Now what?'

'Faramond's sure to be cooking something, wherever he is. Find smoke and we shall find Faramond.'

Faramond was camped in what had once been the central plaza of the city. It was now just a patch of forest with trees growing amid what was left of the paving stones. Between a tree and the statue of some long-dead king, he'd rigged a hammock, and above this was a rectangle of tent cloth to keep the rain off. He was roasting a bird about the size of a pigeon over his fire, and was surrounded by the bones and body parts from the previous night's meal. At the sight of his visitors, he lurched to his feet and backed away.

'Great and glorious Lady, welcome!' he said, holding up his hands then bowing.

'Spare me the pleasantries, Faramond. You are not a pleasant person and neither am I,' said Elvar. 'I have brought you a present.'

She tossed the end of the tether to Faramond, but he raised his hands again and backed away.

'Mighty and fearsome, Ladyship, I need no apprentice,' he mumbled.

'Nonsense, a pig in a pigsty would look after himself better than you. You can have Winston or you can have my displeasure. Which will it be?'

Faramond bowed low. Elvar raised one hand and beckoned to a horseman behind her. He rode forward and dropped Winston's sword, knife, bow, quiver of arrows and boar spear to the ground.

'Ladyship, I am not worthy,' pleaded Faramond.

'Make no mistake, you are a greedy, slovenly, incompetent excuse for a wizard, and you are being punished. This apprentice is your punishment.'

Without another word Elvar turned her horse and re-joined the riders of her escort.

'Go away!' cried Faramond, once he and Winston were alone.

'But Master—'

'I'm not your master. Go!' said the wizard. He pointed a gnarled finger at the horizon and when Winston didn't move, he snatched the remains of a feral chicken and flung it at Winston, who deftly dodged.

'Please, Master. Give me a chance. I can catch boars and roast them for you.'

'I'd rather eat worms!'

Winston traced a spell in the air, then clapped over it to launch the spell. He swayed a little from the effort.

'What did you just cast?' demanded Faramond.

'I just summoned a boar for your eating pleasure.'

'Summoned a boar? You can't just summon a *boar*, you need to know its name. Do you speak boar? Are you on first-name terms with any of the boars in this city? You needed to specify the closest boar.'

'I just traced the spell for *boar* and—'

'You *what?*' screamed Faramond. 'Run for your life!'

Faramond ran for the statue to which one end of his hammock was tied. Winston climbed the tree at the other end just as a horde of boars burst forth through the surrounding greenery. They squealed and grunted as they leapt for Faramond and Winston. Faramond clambered into the gesturing arms of the king's statue, looking like an enormous, bearded baby prince. The boars slashed and tore at his hammock and trampled his campsite.

'Don't just sit in that tree, kill them!' screamed Faramond.

'But Master, my weapons are down on the ground.'

'Stupid, stupid boy, don't you ever think ahead?'

'Fear not, Master. I have a cunning plan.'

Winston traced another spell, spoke a word of fabrication, then cast it toward Faramond. All at once, every boar in the clearing clustered around the base of the statue, leaping, squealing and snapping at the wizard. Although weakened by the two castings, Winston climbed down his tree, fetched his bow and arrows, and climbed back up again.

'Every pig in the place is after me!' shouted Faramond. 'What did you just do?'

'I cast the essence of *delictiar fugoris* at you as a distraction.'

'Idiot boy, you turned me into the world's biggest truffle!' cried Faramond.

'Just for three or four hours, Master, while I recover enough strength to string my bow and shoot one of the boars for your dinner.'

'Three or four *hours*?'

Winston settled down on a branch, took a book from his backpack, and opened it at the bookmark. It was a very fine day, he was home again, Faramond was furious with him, and all was right with the world.

More great reading from Ford Street Publishing

THE WARLOCK'S CHILD

READ ALL SIX BOOKS

THE BURNING SEA	April
DRAGONFALL MOUNTAIN	May
THE IRON CLAW	June
TRIAL BY DRAGONS	July
VOYAGE TO MORTICAS	August
THE GUARDIANS	September

When two of Australia's most popular fantasy authors collaborate, *The Warlock's Child* weaves a new and exciting brand of magic.

RRP $12.95

PAUL COLLINS & SEAN McMULLEN

www.fordstreetpublishing.com **FORD ST**